I0698859

DIMENSIONS OF TIME

Copyright © 2026 by Lance Dakota

All rights reserved. This book or any portion thereof may not be reproduced or used in any manner whatsoever without the express written permission of the publisher except for the use of brief quotation in a book review.

ISBN: 978-1-971940-04-5 Paperback
ISBN: 978-1-971940-05-2 Ebook

Rev. date: 02/10/2026

DIMENSIONS OF TIME

LANCE DAKOTA

LANCE DAKOTA–BIO

Lance Dakota's Novels offer a unique blend of Spirituality and Realism. Each story is designed to inspire readers, encouraging them to navigate life's rising challenges with Faith, Perseverance, and Determination. Lance Dakota's stories resonate with mainstream audiences encompassing passionately- driven Christian based stories and film projects that push boundaries while exploring all forms of human emotions and experiences connected to a journey of an ultimate spiritual growth and enlightenment. Lance Dakota is an award winning author having penned numerous acclaimed articles and a screenwriter, having won "Best Screenplay" Honors in screenplay competitions spanning entertainment centers, such as, New York, Los Angeles, Las Vegas, and London. In addition to his accomplishments in writing, Lance is an accomplished educator, having served as an administrator on every level for over 38-years, holding a Doctorate Degree in Educational Administration, a Master's Degree in Education, and a Bachelor's Degree in Education from Temple University in which he participated on Temple's Nationally ranked wrestling team. Through his success in education, he has been published in numerous research journals, magazines, and newspaper columns, along with being featured in school success stories in news articles, including the New York Times, radio shows, and Nationally Syndicated T.V. Programs. In his free time, Lance enjoys hiking with his husky, Apollo, and volunteering at his Church.

DIMENSIONS OF TIME–ACKNOWLEDGEMENTS

There are many people who have supported me through the years in the pursuit of my dream of writing. My one dear friend, who has been by my side for almost three decades, is my rock in regard *to not giving up* and *maintaining faith* in God while encouraging me to explore the deepest callings within me. Recently, she has endured many trials of her own on just about every level. Yet, she has survived, coming out of these challenges with an enormous amount of evolving strength, grace, and a spiritual-driven mantra of perseverance, involving her own journey toward a greater sense of purpose and enlightenment. The energy, beauty, and force within her has guided me on my quest of creating faith-based stories that have a purpose and a message that can resonate along with serving as a pathway in helping one find their destiny; the deepest parts of ourselves, the ultimate truth, that we are often afraid to explore and embrace. With this sense of exploration and unyielding realm of confidence, resonating from our Lord Jesus Christ, *the ultimate Truth*–I would like to sincerely thank, my friend and confidant, Norell for all of her on- going, unwavering love, support, and encouragement, forthwith, placing a belief in me that we can, truly, clasp upon and take hold of a distant shooting star… If we truly just BELIEVE…

To Channel and her two sons, Christian and Brandon, who have given me so much throughout my lifetime, I am sincerely thankful that I have been able to travel along the way with all of you as your Godfather and, in a way, your Guardian Angel, of sorts. All of you mean so much to me and I am so proud. I am proud of what you have become and all the goals you have accomplished. I have watched you grow to much more than I ever could imagine and I love you more than you will ever know. Stay close to God, always pray, and always know that I will be forever by your sides, guarding you, supporting you, protecting you. Life can be difficult. But, Life is a gift from God. His Son, Jesus, is our True Savior and Protector. In Him we should trust. For He is pure, He is Noble, He is the one who has given up His life, the ultimate sacrifice, so that we may live in the arms of God. John 3:16–"For God so loved the world, that he gave his only Son, that whoever believes in Him should not perish but have eternal life."

To my sister, Patti, the greatest writer I have ever known, thank you for your collaboration and belief in this story, "Nephilim's Sun." Your belief in the book and film mean so much to me. Your quiet nature and enormous Faith has helped me stay on the true path toward His purpose and fate for who I should become and where I should be. Your exemplary talents in writing will serve as a Light for His ministry in which many souls will be saved and the power of Light over Darkness will prevail. John 8:12–"When Jesus spoke again to the people, he said, "I am the Light of the world. Whoever follows me will never walk in darkness, but will have the Light of life." Keep writing… Keep praying… Keep being who He wants you to be…

Dedication

For my sister, Patti.

According to astrophysicists, Grey Aliens, Zeta Reticulan, account for many client abductions. They possess humanlike small bodies, smooth grey–colored skin, and elongated heads. Modern- day accounts of alien abductions began in the 1950's with cases such as with Betty and Barney Hill in 1961. Abductees often experience similar themes, including memories of medical examinations and various communications with aliens. Several of these abductees said they were taken from their homes and vehicles. These abductions usually occurred at night.

Their experiences of being taken frequently involved a sense of paralysis, unable to move, bright beams of light, and missing time. The UFO's interiors were described by a abductees as being metallic. Some abductees reported seeing other humans aboard the UFO's along with various types of humanlike hybrids. The communication with the aliens usually involved telepathic processes with no spoken words. The states that experience the most UFO sightings and claimed abductions include, Alaska, Nevada, Colorado, Pennsylvania, New York, and Arizona. Some famous cases of UFO's and alien abductions include:

The Roswell Case in 1947 involving a crashed UFO and alien survivors that spurred on alien theories and claims in the decades that followed.

Project Blue Book, a Governmental Agency, that investigated thousands of claimed cases of UFO sightings and alien abductions.

Crop Circles often have been linked to UFO sightings along withe blood-drained cattle.

The Antonio Villas Boas Abduction that occurred in the 1950's on a farm in Brazil.

The Betty and Barney Hill abductions case that occurred in 1961 in New Hampshire.

The Betty Andreasson Luca Abduction, shortly after the Hill's, in which she claimed she was experimented on by aliens in various ways aboard their ship.

The Pascagoula abduction case in 1973, involving two men, Charles Hickson and Calvin Parker, who claimed to have been taken by robotic type of aliens.

The Travis Walton's abduction case that occurred in 1975 in which he claimed to have been taken for five days.

The Allagash Waterway abduction in 1976 involved four men who claimed they were abducted while camping in Maine.

Witnesses of Alien ShapeShifters, who can change their appearance, theorized by some to appear human and deceive others as part of an underlying secret strategy to infiltrate the human race, world leadership, and pave the way for hybrid offspring.

xi

CHAPTER 1
Reflection upon the Glass

S edona, Arizona (Present Day). I enter my bedroom before the colored draped mountains of my family's ranch and sit down by a large open bay window, feeling the warmth of a strange breeze, seemingly cast out through a rainbow prism, colors of time. Leaning my bare arms with small scars on my forearms upon the window's ledge, I blankly gaze out toward the mountain range while reaching into the far edges of my mind held within a distant tint of a blue, purple haze, emanating from a fading sun; a fading memory I had hoped to breathe away, years ago, letting these *image of Grey's* painstakingly slip from my traumatic, convulsive-driven grasp.

I'll never forget. But, *I'll never remember,* I keep telling myself, as I continue to gaze out toward an unusual sun, pushing *it* back even past my darkest thoughts of the most secret part of my mind. For almost two decades, I had learned to adjust, not even giving it a name. I refer to it as *it, that, what,* but never by a *name.* If I did, I was afraid *it, that, what,* would resurrect to the fore-front part of my brain, emerging from the grey into the images of slanted, black, oval darkened eyes, mixing with my emotional thoughts of the past within my cerebellum, tossing me into a reawakening of contemptuous dark force driven by the arms of reality–pulling me back out *that* open window, *that* night. I am trying to forget… But, how can one forget that of which is burned within the flesh. Therapists call it, *Repression.* I call it, *Survival,* the name of the name of an emotional strategy I feel safe holding onto, at least for now. Yet, after all these years, I believe it is time to finally let it go. It's funny. People pay a lot of money to try to remember while I pay a lot of money to forget… hoping to cast out those darkened memories of thought back into the far edges of the universe.

Taking out my journal, the one I titled, Dimensions of Time the one my therapist suggested I begin to write, even through my objections, although fearful of *that* moment in time coming alive again in the present, even if only briefly as a healing tool upon the blank pages before me; clasping upon courage, somewhere hidden far within myself, my fist tightens upon the pen, I take a deep breath and transcend into a quiet, hallow gasp of terrified silence as I being to remember, *That Night…It, That, What, Oh my God, Them…*

I glance over to an aquarium with a large pet tree iguana, staring at me, watching… and with a flash of light, I vanish back into the memory…upward through a dark, yet, illuminated tunnel toward some kind of elongated vessel, hovering… I remember being placed onto a cold, hard slab by them, totally naked, being stretched out and bound by my wrists and ankles on my back with a bulb of purple light pulsating above me, suddenly feeling the cold slab turn hot.

Looking up, I see their reptilian yellow eyes, as a *reflection upon the glass* as with the aquarium, the iguana staring at me with as strange turn ward cast of his dark slanted eyes. I can see them looking down at me as if I am the one in the aquarium, staring down at me through the glass, reflections appearing with an echo, the watchers peering in. Frightened, scared, sensing something was going to emerge from the stillness of them standing over me, I attempt to struggle, to push my wide parted bare legs together, bound wide apart to each corner of the increasingly hot slab withy arms outstretched wide overtop my head, leaving only the expression of my eyes to react to their on-going cold stares amidst the rising heat beneath me. My nipples tingle to an unseen touch with an enhanced sensation pulsing with the pulsing light above me as my toes curl, digging into seemingly small granular rocks, as I begin to wonder, just wondering with my growing cascading fear.

Suddenly, there is a loud sound, some kind of engine, as they abruptly turn their attention away from me. Briefly, a grey hand with elongated fingers appears to lock a latch of glass around me, and then… vanishes. My arms are set free. They drop, dangling over the metallic table. I rise up as the bounds on my ankles seem to melt, sinking my feet into granular stone sands of an aquarium, pleasing out through the alien aquarium purple hazes shield of glass. I watch as they lead other naked captives, mostly young women, down a long illuminated purple glazed hallway, down into darkness, fading as a bad memory; continuing to try to forget… I look up, away from my journal, away from this cascading dark images within my mind, and wonder, just wondering. All of a sudden, out of nowhere, that grey hand re-appears and reaches out with his elongated fingers–These fingers tightly grip my bare shoulder, pulling me back through the dark tunnel to where it all began…

It was Fall, 2001, when it happened. I was just finishing up my last year at NYU, majoring in journalism and minoring in local activism–to save the planet, right after 911. The city was beginning to come to grasp with what happened as I, too, felt I was beginning a new era. During this emerging era in my life, I, *Idealistic* and *Innocent* Maria Rivera, wanted to change the world, hoping for a new beginning for both the city of New York and myself, thinking somehow that we were connected and if I could change myself, then the rest of the city and world would follow. As I gazed out the high-rise building of our fifteenth floor apartment bedroom window on the *West Side* of Manhattan, looking through my telescope, the sun arose in the distance with mesmerizing colors, cascading atop rippling reflections of the Hudson River, winding around glistening skyscrapers, much different than the mountain ridges on my family farm in Sedona, Arizona, and yet, in some peculiar way, they were the same. My fist tightened around my Red Rosary Beads, adjusting *my lens* and focusing in on a strange elongated object, hovering above the Hudson as a wall clock above me was ticking–8:33 am.

My best friend, Crystal, like a sister to me, and I moved to New York, about a year prior, in search of our dreams and other dreams deep within ourselves that we were unaware we even had. I still remember my father, a decorated fighter pilot and research scientist, encouraging us to *push full throttle toward our targets* and, what I refer to as seeking out or destinies hidden within the *East Side* of our souls, a place we didn't plan on residing, however, yearning to know what it was like to live there. Yet, while I just dreamed of the *East Side, involving my repressed sexual desires and fantasies,* Crystal, aka *the wild-side sister,* visited there often, fully aware of her own unapologetic *reputation-based airspace.* She *flew* without restriction, inhibition, nor malice. She just… flew.

As I watched this new sunrise through our apartment window with this new valley of hope before me, I sensed the rebirth of a city rising from a deep winter's sleep, shaking off snowy images of ice storms that shut it down, in some instances, for days at a time. Now, flowery landscapes in parks began to blossom with the essence of a reborn energy encapsulated by a bustling city life. Cars that haven't moved from their spots in months, echoed out sounds of engines turning over, coughing, and tumbling, spitting out exhaust – arising eerily, as if twirling, dancing, upward toward our open window within this captured moment in the visible space/time continuum of our reality.

"Well, there's a dichotomy, Rosary beads and a sexy cheerleader outfit," Crystal laughed out, causing me to abruptly turn. For a brief moment, I saw *an older image of myself.* "Come on. We're going to be late. If you want a ride, you're going to have to hurry up and change into your real costume," Crystal added, running a towel through her short cropped wet red hair, just having gotten out of the shower, covered in a mini towel with a "Full Throttle," Air Force insignia.

"I am ready," I confidently snipped back, flipping back my long blonde hair, wearing a skimpy bare mid-drift Dallas Cowboy Cheerleader Jersey #77 and a sheer cheeky white boy- short, my pink thong, like my emerging courage–transparent through *it, what I've been searching for on the East Side within me.*

The elongated object rose, suddenly, seemingly moving toward me. I let out a slight gasp as Crystal dropped the towel to change into her own costume. Completely nude, she began searching through the bin. As she did, she glanced up and noticed my pink thong through my transparent sheer, white, tight short shorts.

"Cute thong… Looks like that's all you have on," Crystal said, jokingly, adding, "Where did you get that costume, anyway, Frederick's of Hollywood?"

"No. I found it, in that bin with all of your other slutty whore outfits… You know the window's open?"

Crystal laughed, "I don't care," she said, digging into the blue bin. "I, totally, forgot about that cheerleader outfit. Was really drunk when I wore it. Couldn't remember anything about that night…" Crystal found her costume and began putting it on.

"Sometimes that's a good thing, right? Not remembering?"

I pulled back the telescope, upward, arching my head back…

"I can't believe it's Halloween already with everything that's happened." "Well, Time is relative, even for the city of Manhattan."

"Says my Einstein, sister. What are you searching for anyway, some distant alien, a man, or maybe… a woman?"

"Yeah, right." I volleyed back, zooming in on the strange elongated object. "How do you know what you… like if you never…"

"Why do you always have to bring that up? No. Right now, I'm just focused on my research." I adjusted my telescope, focusing closer in on the strange object.

"Well, you're twenty-one years old and still doing research."

Suddenly, the object flew off, vanishing. I turned away from the telescope and there it was, Crystal dressed in an alien costume – LARGE HEAD, SLANTED BLACK EYES, LONG GREY FINGERS.

I gasped… She looked soooo real. "Wow. I didn't see that one in your bin," I said, stunned. My spine tensed, those fingers. Briefly, I imagined them touching me… I shook off the darkened thought, moving away from the window and dimensional dreams of far off universes, back toward the safety of my bed. Sitting down upon it, I began gazing into a small mirror upon a table next to a straw cowboy hat, wondering what world I should explore next…

"Come on. Go get changed into your real costume," Crystal said with more of a commanding voice. "You know you're not going to wear that."

"No," I replied again, adding, "I want to…experience something different, today," as I opened up the drawer to the table, pulling out make-up and glancing deeper into the small mirror within me.

"Yesterday, you wanted to be a nun. What happened?" Crystal stated, confused, adding, "So, you're actually going to go outside like that…"

"Yeah. Why not?" I replied, opening a golden tube of lipstick with an one-hundred-eighty degree angle affirmative twist.

"Because that's not you," Crystal threw up her hands, moving her slanted black eyes out of place, adding, while adjusting her *Grey Alien look,* "Besides, there can't be two wild sisters. We balance each other out, like one of Einstein's equations… right?"

Meticulously putting on the bright red lipstick and lip liner, I *aligned* Crystal back into her place with a brush of blush. "You put on an alien outfit and, all of a sudden, you become intrigued with the universe, making parallel exertions about quantum physics?"

"Wow. It's like we've changed bodies or something. You're the whore and, now, I'm the genius," Crystal sarcastically countered, her black slanted eyes sliding back into place.

"You're imagining another dichotomy," I responded while gazing at myself in the mirror. "I think you're jumping dichotomies," Crystal said with a forced laugh. "What are you doing?" Crystal asked, breaking me out of my trance, looking within, the other side of myself in the mirror.

"What does it look like I'm doing?" I responded, pausing, putting on thick make-up as a means to transcend myself through the portal to the *East Side.*

"Like you're trying to decide if you're going out that door and into the world as a whore or a nun," Crystal said with a grin, pointing toward the partially open apartment door.

I glanced over, shook my head, turned back, and resumed putting on make-up.

"I'm just putting on make-up, not deciding on my persona for the day. Anyway, it's Halloween, isn't it? You can be whatever you want to be."

"Yes, and yesterday you wanted to be a nun, sista Maria."

"Well, things change," I stated what I thought was a Philosophical summation of my life. "Not that quickly," Crystal added another variable to the equation I believed, at that time, made sense. Why not explore? Explore the unknown… Isn't that what humanity is all about? "You don't even wear make-up," she added. Damn, another variable. I found myself doing new math, scientifically based sequences on a quantum level that could…well, create a massive explosion. But, I kept going, taking my first step out that new persona door…

"There's a first time for everything, right?" I threw out another trite, not well thought out, response, just as the experience I was about to lay out for my day – *not well thought out… more thrilled, excited at showing off and getting attention…* With my heavy make-up, I turned toward Crystal. "So, how do I look?"

Crystal smiled and shook her head, "Like a sista from another universe, preparing to be probed and researched."

"Cool," I said flipping back my hair with a nod. "Maybe they'll find something I didn't know existed," I added, bending down and pulling out a pair of high white boots from underneath my bed… Shorter than a miniskirt, my butt cheeks teased being exposed in which the slightest vertical downward movement of my upper torso or upward flow of a slight breeze could possibly embarrassingly reveal my pink heart thong panties. Even so, I stubbornly began to put on the pair of boots to emphasize my debate position. My sister, although she was younger than me, always seem to win every argument. I pulled them on. Rising, I stamped them into place, turned, and looked at myself in a larger, coming to life, larger full-length mirror. I smiled in self- approval at my new look, the new me, my new persona with one foot out the door and… posed.

"See? Ready." I stood, confidently, in my boots and new found persona, pulling slightly down on the hem of my Dallas Cowboy Cheerleader #77 Jersey, not thinking enough ahead that I had to actually go outside and possibly flash my lower butt cheeks with *that* slight breeze or jarring turn just to prove a *Don't Rush Me point*. I wondered how many other young women in revealing outfits were going to do so, today, to just win an argument.

"You're really going like that?" She responded, mockingly, looking at me up and down with a surprised smile. I nodded in an affirmed manner, yet hesitantly while grabbing hold of a short jean jacket, putting it on as if that would help cover the rest of me, the below the waist part.

"Okay, whore," she laughed out loud, befittingly labeling me for the moment while adding, "It's amazing you're still a virgin."

Yes! She said it aloud with my outfit echoing secret desires from within. Twenty one- years-old and I still hadn't *opened my window*. Back in Arizona, I had a couple of long-term relationships. However, they were more like friends. I never really was attracted, *in that way,* to either of them. Maybe it was my Catholic upbringing–*To stay a virgin until you are married.*

Yet, my sister wasn't much like me. She didn't follow church doctrine, kind of like the place within myself that I didn't want to admit I wanted to visit – the *Fifty Shades of Grey East Side* neighborhood place like other women who read that book, you know. Ugh. I'm glad no one is able to hear my thoughts. But, it's true. I wanted to be taken away from the *safety of my bed on my boring East Side…* and one night, as if my thoughts were sent out into the universe as a probe deep into space… it happened.

Crystal with her smile, took a pic of me seductively posing into the full-length mirror. "Well, that should do it," she said after snapping a few more pics.

"Do what?" I responded, doing another sexy, cute pose, sticking out my bare bottom cheeks with a twist of my swaying hips.

"Attract whatever it is you're searching for… to research you," Crystal tossed me the straw cowboy hat. I caught it and put it on.

As Crystal and I were walking out the door, I glanced back, not knowing that my life was about to drastically change with the most important part of my life about to rise as the colors out the window, hovering over the Hudson. I felt like a blossoming rose, hesitant to allow a secret version of myself come out and, at the same time, excited to go down a path I never explored before. Like our father said, "Full throttle ahead."

I took a breath and veered my fighter jet of my soul out that partially open door—leaving my nun's outfit behind, just me and my cute, skimpy outfit… the telescope mysteriously turned…

As a little girl, my father stood by my side. He always stood by my side with his quiet strength and demeanor, never letting me venture too far off on my own while letting me explore my own paths of the unknown. From a very early age, I became fascinated with space, what is beyond the dimensional constraints of time that seemingly keep us bound to this area of the universe. I remember him telling me that if you take one spec of sand and call that, "Earth." And then take all the specs of sand on that beach and all the beaches in the world—There are more suns and planets in the universe than all these specs of sand. It made me think, are we the only life forms in this universe? And if not, where are the others? Do they believe in God and are a part of His Will? My father's words resonated with me, especially the ones he spoke of from the Word of God. Each night, as the sun was setting in the distance, he would read to me the Bible, keeping me magnetized to the stories within it. My father had a way of making the Bible come alive. Throughout my life, I could actually feel these stories, the messages, as if each heart beat sounded out through sands of time…

Now, I was about to explore a parallel universe, one in which one's alternate self exists, the opposite of who we are within this reality. I always felt the opposite me. Yet, I always turned away from her, afraid to become what I fantasied to be. Hesitant to blend the lines of reality and cross into that other dimension of an alternate universe. As I drove with Crystal in my new found persona of this parallel existence, I imagined standing on a beach, reaching down, and picking up a handful of sand, letting it flow down through the palm of my hand…

CHAPTER 2
An Image within the Sun

As Crystal drove through NYU's campus, I sat, clinging to the passenger's side door, pressing my bare legs tightly together, pulling my straw cowboy hat down over my eyes while gazing out at all the students, professors, just about everyone walking through the campus.

"Am I really going to do this?" I asked myself, beginning to question my critical decision back at our apartment. "Maybe I should have kept all of this just a fantasy…" I thought, and maybe there was a reason that telescope turned. It was as if another universe was turning my personality inside/out, a mirrored reflection of what I, myself, cast out from that small mirror which I used to put my make-up on. I had transformed myself, emerged myself into a series of equations that I didn't know the answers to, yet yearned to discover.

I pulled down the visor of Crystal's car, and glanced into its small mirror. It was as if dimensional time had followed me within reflections of my inner-self. My red lipstick was meticulously in place. The game board was set. My breaths became shortened and fast, pushing the visor back up and staring out toward the campus and into a new world…

"Are you going to get out? Or What?" Crystal asked while adjusting the radio.

"Maybe this wasn't such a good idea," I responded, adding, "I think I want to go back… get the nun outfit. Play it safe."

"There's no going back, now, sista from another universe. You've already launched into space in your new sexy persona." Crystal laughed out, reaching toward her glove compartment. Taking out a joint, she lit it up and held it up toward me.

"What's that?" I said, naively.

"It's for you. Here, inhale some courage, whore," Crystal affirmed pressing it closer into my comfort zone. I hesitated. "Come on. You know you want to," she said with a mischievous smile.

I looked back out toward the campus. There were several students dressed in costumes, but nothing like the revealing one I was wearing. I began to feel very vulnerable, almost naked, then with another puff, completely nude, sitting in the seated position with barely any remnants of the white short shorts visible from where I viewed them. So, I grabbed hold, tightly, of the joint and took a couple of deeper puffs, not wanting to let go, and another…

"Easy. You don't want to get too stoned while in your hot outfit," Crystal snipped, taking the joint back, forcibly from my hand. "That's how I ended up in, well, situations."

Turning, I noticed a group of students in costumes, staring upward into a glaring sun. "I wonder what they're looking at?" I said with a couple of coughs of partial remnants of the joint.

"Who cares? Just get out. Go explore your wild side, sista," Crystal directed, reaching past me and opening the passenger side door.

With a slight push, I slid out of my seat, the white boy short riding up even further, exposing most of my bottom's cheeks and out into a wondrous, vast, beautiful universe. As I stood alone in the face of a bright, sun, I spanned looking at the campus full of students, and many, many others, open and vulnerable to all of them. Before I could gasp and turn back, Crystal sped away… at light speed like a comet.

I stood alone, born by a creation of thick make-up and short shorts into a new universe.

Tossing my backpack, my past life as a researcher, securely on my back behind me, I began walking as one who was going to become the "researched subject," across the campus as heads turned, inquisitively and seductively staring at me. Guys, and a couple of girls, gave me flirtatious nods and smiles, as I attempted to keep my head down and move forward, moving into this new version of my self, morphing into that of an exploratory, intense sexuality-driven new "norm."

As I walked with my new persona, across the campus, "The War of the Worlds" 1938 Radio Broadcast by Orson Welles, echoed through the campus grounds…

Suddenly, there is a similar strange echo in the sky as a small group of students attempt to glance up into the glaring sun. One student in the group was dressed as a wizard as he pointed his magical appearing staff upward, toward what appeared to be a large, long cylindrical grey object, hovering. This wizard gestured to a female student dressed as a Tolkien Hobbit, clinging next to him as if captivated by some sort of medieval wizardry force as the head of the staff glistened against the backdrop of the glistening object, blending into the sky in some kind of weird dimensional driven intergalactic phenomenon. The wizard had unusual long blond hair.

"See? It's right up there," the wizard exclaimed with a certain level of excitement to her. "What do you think it is, Julius?" the hobbit responded, obediently.

"Don't know. It looks really strange, but very, very beautiful..." he said, looking down and staring at me approaching as I played it off, acting like I didn't notice. I just kept walking toward them as if being beamed up into some mystical force from a celestial unknown planet. Landing I asked, "So, what's everyone looking at?" I look up, too, but can't see anything except for shimmering bright metallic silver, glistening in the sun that is too bright as the wizard kept staring, infatuatedly and lustfully at me with his hobbit appearing to become jealous.

"There's something up there," she responded to me in a forced-like directed manner. "It's hard to see. Sun's too bright," she added in a more normal tone. "I've got to get to class. Are you coming, Julius?" she asked the wizard with a cast of a concerned jealous-driven look.

The wizard, still staring at me, unable to take his eyes off my legs as if he was trying to decide what kind of spell he would like to cast upon me, hesitated to the hobbit's demand of an immediate answer. Smiling in a kind of that weird way, the wizard stared at me, nodded, and blew me a kiss, lowering is his erect staff as he followed her, silently, without a word—although appearing not willingly inboxing me with a thousand words within his look toward me... watching me as they disappeared behind a bell tower.

That left me alone again in this strange alternative universe that I created by flipping personas, after other students dispersed, glancing up into the bright morning's sun, a move that would open a new dimension to my life, the one I was in control of, until this point of my travels. I pulled down my straw cowboy hat over my eyes, and walked further into the small mirror of my mind as I attempted to figure out what was still hovering above me.

Then, with another echo–*it* happened.

"Here, try these," a deep, powerful man's voice echoed, pulling me back down from looking up. I became startled, not at *what* was above me, but at *what* was before me as he reached out to hand me peculiar metallic appearing sunglasses. He was a very tall man, slim, but really fit, about 6'5" wearing an attractive peculiar grey suit and gloves. His eyes, although human, appeared with a reflective-tint of yellow, kind of, in a way reptilian-esque, and yet, he was gorgeous. Not just pictures in magazines gorgeous. I mean, gorgeous, gorgeous and you can tell he had money, my own Christian Grey. My mind sank to his deep hallow voice and mesmerizing grey-yellow eyes. As I connected with him, he reached and took hold of the sunglasses, feeling though briefly, a spark.

"Are you okay?" He said, gently caressing my cheek (in my mind), as I remain stunned, frozen, staring at him like a possum caught in the cross hairs of the beams of car headlights.

"Yes. I am," I responded back with the best wit I had at that moment, shaking myself out of his trance, away from the high beams, trying to act, now, like I barely noticed him. I came to New York to find my dream and here he was, standing right in front of me.

I put the sunglasses on and stared back up at the sky, wanting, though, to stare back down to him, the fantasy man of my dreams.

"Nice makeup. How did you get your eyes to look like that?" I asked, still somewhat startled at his sudden appearance and his… costume. He just smiled and stared at me as I put the sunglasses on and looked back up at the sky, wanting, though, to stare back down at him – A flock of birds, appearing as a cylindrical object.

"Oh… I thought it was something else…" Taking the sunglasses off, I looked back down. The strange man, before me with his mesmerizing eyes, was gone, vanished as if he had melted away into an envelope laced dimensional fold. "Where did he go?" I thought, in a bewildered and disappointed way, feeling drawn to him, wanting to have had discovered more, the research astrophysicist part of me kicking in, as I reached back and pulled my wedgie out in my sexy outfit. Confused, I continued walking though NYU, wondering, just wondering what I had just encountered. I would attend classes, that day, trying to concentrate on the lectures. However, I would continually be drawn back to that brief moment, gazing into his beautiful grey-yellow eyes, my toes curling while feeling uncontrollable tingles up and down my spine, imagining a hand with long fingers caressingly moving upward upon my, shockingly, extending thigh...

Later, I would write in NYU's Newspaper Column–*Something unusual flew by the campus of NYU, earlier today. Several people witnessed a large oval shaped object, with lights and seemingly no propulsion system fly off at a high-speed after appearing to hover over the campus for a few minutes. University officials had no comment on what the object may have been. Some said it was a flock of birds. Some said, something else...*

The Bell Tower of the university sounded out, scattering the birds, flying overhead into distant cries blending with scattering echoes of my peculiar thoughts within my mind.

Appearing, as the birds disappeared flying off, female soccer players dressed as zombies, wearing yellow soccer jersey's with large leopard, black spots, passed me by. As they did, a few began to hit on me... especially one. She was tall, well built, strong looking, with green dyed hair.

"Hey, nice outfit, love," she said to me, pausing, towering over me, adding, "I'm looking for a new side-kick." She reached out, brushed back my hair, and gently caressed my shoulder. Briefly, I felt a tingle from her touch, a sensation I had never felt before. With a downward cast of my eyes, I smiled at her, signaling acceptance yet caution, and quickly turned away. Honoring my signal, she smiled, nodded, and stepped back, letting me pass as my long blonde hair flowed through her fingertips from her touch on my shoulder... The Bell Tower sounded out again and again... But, I did not turn back even in a glance, fearful I would fall for her. So, I walked away, simply walked away through the campus, not looking back as I continued to feel her touch, an unique tingling sensation with each echoing sound of a bell...

RING... A small bell sounds out, dangling by the entrance of the university student bookstore. I entered, paused, and looked around. A peculiar female cashier in a Viking costume, glanced over at me. I nodded. "Let me know if you need any help with anything," the cashier with large horns, nodded back while, strangely, watching me as I went over to a shelf, searching for tights. Okay... I still felt exposed, not only in my very revealing outfit, but also apparently what was churning within me, like I was searching for something deep inside myself. I always was searching, for that black hole in space, a new planet, an unforeseen emerging solar system- oh, and love. That was the hardest to find out of all of them and a telescope didn't help me, up until, now. I searched through the shelf of tights reflecting upon that gray-haired zombie's touch.

Suddenly, THE POT KICKED IN as I felt dizzy and dazed, the room swaying. Looking for anything to keep me from falling, I leaned up against a post next to the shelf. Out of the corner of my eye, I could still see the cashier watching me… now, there were two vikings, admiring me like I was in a foreign land about to be conquered, readying their longships. I envisioned being captured, stripped nude; my wrists, ankles tied to a stake, and being carried off by rough appearing warriors upside down horizontally and lifted up as cargo into their boat.

I tried to fight the effects of the pot. Yet, the more I tried, the more I felt vulnerable and lost control of even my thoughts… They began tying me to the mast of the ship…

RING. My phone rang. I answered. "Hey Crystal," I spoke before hearing my sister's voice as a siren from the sea.

"You sound distracted. Are you in class yet?" Crystal asked.

"No," I answered, regaining myself, breaking free and dashing off that *Viking Longship,* and heading to the dressing room, my wrists unbound and tights, a symbol of safety, in hand. "Where are you?" She asked, sensing my confusion.

"In the bookstore…" I confessed, looking for a dressing room door that was unlocked. "Why are you in the bookstore?" Crystal let out a laugh, adding, "I think I know why." "You got me. I'm getting a pair of tights," I ended my confession.

"I knew you'd pull the rip cord," Crystal said with another blurted out chuckle.

The bookstore dangling doorway bell, rang out, again. I looked up. The female zombie soccer players entered the bookstore, scattering about, like the birds in the sky.

"Well, did you at least get the attention you were searching for?" Crystal asked.

The zombies moved, methodically within the aisles, encircling me with their black spots of jerseys, becoming more prominent with each movement, like leopards encircling their prey.

"Too much attention," I replied, adding, "That's why I'm changing. Feel vulnerable, like I'm some sort of prey or something."

"I thought that was the look you were going for? To be the prey…" Crystal confirmed my subconscious voice within.

"Okay. You're right. I should have just worn the nun costume," I said, adding, "So now what? Do you want me to do penance for pretending to be a whore?" I sarcastically ended.

"Only if you want to, sista Maria," Crystal jokingly replied, adding, "I'm always right. You know that, especially about worlds I live in. Your world, my dear, is in another part of the universe. I'm always right…"

"Not always…Maybe I won't wear the tights," I attempted to regain some self- reassurance within my annoying subconscious whore voice.

"Well, anyway, whatever you decide, be careful. Guys can be really aggressive." "Not guys," I said, noticing the zombies moving closer to me from amidst the aisles.

"Actually, women…zombies."

"Really? Well, I heard, somewhere, that zombies make great lovers…" The green haired zombie approached me… I slightly gasped as she smiled.

"Are you sure you're not gay?" Crystal asked, adding, "I mean, it's okay if you are. I always thought it would be cool to have a gay sister."

"Would you stop saying that?" I nervously said with the green haired zombie standing before me.

"Well, don't you attract what you put out there, in the universe? Isn't that part of your quantum physics or something?" Crystal continued her role as an amateur astrophysicist.

The green haired zombie, softly, slowly, reached out and began stroking my long blonde hair. She smiled again, kissed me on the cheek, stroked my hair, and continued on down the aisle, turning away from me.

"I'm not sure what I'm attracting, right now," I said to Crystal, adding, attempting to find a dressing room door that was unlocked, "Don't feel like myself… Everything feels foggy. Got to go. Sorry…" Finding one, I frantically ducked into the empty dressing room, pulling the door shut behind me. Quickly, not knowing what was going to happen next upon this strange day, I kicked off my boots and pulled down my boy-short to my ankles, and stepped out of them. I held up the tights to put them on – SCREAMS. I peered out of the door – A BRIGHT PULSATING PURPLE LIGHT.

I pulled the door back shut and slid down into a fetal position, clenching the tights to my chest, feeling the beat of my heart, pulsing, beating… as if fading into another dimension.

The screams faded. I looked up and could see a zombie's feet beneath the doorway. The zombie attempted to open it, move the handle. But, thankfully, I had the cognitive awareness to lock it. Then–I heard a click. The door opened – THE GREEN HAIRED ZOMBIE, stood over me, just wearing my football jersey, panties, and cowboy hat, towering in a commanding manner as she entered. She looked down at me beginning to quiver as I attempted to curl up even more.

She reached down and, gently, guided me to my feet. After taking off my cowboy hat and football jersey, she turned me around and pushed me up against a post. I shook, that weird tingle returning, exploding, as she began caressing me – sliding down my legs, my pink thong panty to my ankles… I felt recaptured… tied again to the mast of a ship. The tights fell from my hands as I deeply gasped, feeling her long fingers move up my legs… closing my eyes…

MY PHONE RANG, awakening me. I noticed I was still leaning up against the post by the shelf of tights. I was confused, regaining myself as in my apparent hallucination, I said to myself, "It must be the pot. Yes. I was just hallucinating. That's what it was…"

"Crystal?" I asked, answering my phone.

"You sound distracted. Are you in class, yet?" Crystal asked. "Didn't we have this conversation?" I replied, still bewildered. "What conversation?" Crystal asked.

The cashier approached me, one of my Viking Conquerors, as if brazenly sailing into my coastal region, preparing the breach my defenses, the tights clenched in my hand, to my chest.

"Hold on," I said to Crystal, preparing my battlements.

"Are you alright? Do you want to check out?" The cashier said to me with that same bizarre, inquisitive stare. Silence. She paused as if caught in another dimensional fold as I glanced around the bookstore. No zombies.

"What happened to the people?" I asked, still wondering what had occurred with the purple haze these past few minutes in my own dimension of pot-laced driven attentiveness.

"People?" The cashier asked with a really weird look, adding with an even weirder smile, "There are no…people." The cashier's eyes appeared to change – pupils inverting, yellow…

"Good-bye. I'm out of here," I thought. "Sorry. I've changed my mind. Not what I was looking for." I tossed the cashier the tights with my finger imprinted on it and left, feeling like I had to overcome planetary g-forces to get out of there.

Once outside, feeling a slight breeze return with the escape from the University Twilight Zone, I suddenly realized that I was still wearing my new revealing sexy persona. And yet, I felt surprisingly more secure than with the tights within that strange bookstore.

I looked up, hearing the birds returning, flying overhead and found myself standing in the open campus upon this sunny day with remnants of feeling stoned. I took a sigh of relief, coughed out the past few minutes, and marched on, getting used to my new look and the persona I was allowing to emerge from deep within me. Then, being curious, feeling a presence, I glanced back toward the bookstore, although just briefly. The Viking stood by the window… watching me.

"Maria? Are you still there? Maria?" Crystal said, still waiting on the phone. "Oh…Sorry," I said, bringing my phone closer.

"Why do you sound out of it?" Crystal asked.

"Hey, where did you get that pot?" I replied, somewhat angry, continuing to *strut my stuff* across the campus, noticing guys checking me out. "Why?" Crystal asked.

"I keep imagining things…" I said, glancing back toward the bookstore, the Viking, still by the window. "People watching me."

"Watching? Don't you mean staring? Aren't you wearing a sexy outfit? Of course, they're…watching you," Crystal said, sarcastically with a slight laugh.

"Just forget it," I said turning away, keeping my eyes straight ahead. "Why are you calling me, anyway? Are you coming back to get me?"

"No. You already launched into your orbit, my dear sista. You know why I'm calling," Crystal said, changing to a serious tone.

"Oh, come on, Crystal. This is the third time, this week," I objected, although knowing it was useless and what I would succumb to, as I always did.

"But, you like the going to the library. Look. I'll text you as soon as he leaves," Crystal said. There was always a *he* in Crystal's life, sometimes as many as five. I admired her for that, not so much for having all those men, but as to how she juggled all of them without any of them knowing about the others. She was definitely skillful in keeping them secret toward each other and at the same time, interested.

"Ugh. Sure. Whatever…" I finished my fake objection, knowing how it was going to end. "You're the best! Thanks, whore," Crystal's voice sounded exuberant. "I'll make it up to you. Will call you when he's gone." I hung up. Each time she did this, she never made it up to me.

"Whore?" I thought. This is my new nickname? I shrugged off the thought and startled, I saw the man in the peculiar grey suit watching me, standing by the bell tower smoking a cigar. He returned as he disappeared, without warning, without fanfare, as if slipping in and out of some transportation of consciousness formed by an envelop of a worm hole dimensional fold…

When I entered my astronomy class, it was like entering another galaxy. I could actually feel the coldness of space with Dr. Cummings, the professor, already teaching with a large white board screen in front of the classroom full of students as I made my way toward an empty desk in the back part of this educationally-toned galaxy. The lights were off, only the illuminating light of the screen showing a distant part of the universe as I sat down at the desk, opened my notebook, pressed my legs together, in slight modesty, and strangely sensed a vacuum of darkness.

"Let's take a look, now, at a large galaxy called, Alcyoneus. It's known as a Giant Radio Galaxy…" Dr. Cummings, methodically, in a monotone continued gesturing and pointing toward the illuminated screen of the bright star filled galaxy in Alcyoneus. I knew about Alcyoneus very well. It was one of my favorite galaxies. However, a moved on from it, years ago, being drawn to observing even farther away galaxies at the edge of the universe. So, why was I being drawn back to this one? Why, now?

As I took notes, I glanced up. There, in the front, a student turned around. Within the illuminated light of the screen, with the large Galaxy of Alcyoneus in the background and/or foreground in relation to my seat in the class in the back, was that wizard, smiling at me as if he knew some dark secret of my past. I tried to pretend that I didn't notice him, his weird stare.

"What is he doing in this class?" I thought. "Is he following me? And why is he looking at me like that? Is it my outfit…or something else. I focused in on the screen, the distant galaxy emerging even larger, attempting to distance myself from my thoughts, once again, pressing my bare legs closer together, feeling as if an erupting, stirring volcano, a swaying awareness of being partially naked, then, in a way, completely nude and open before the universe rushing over me.

"Ugh," I thought. "There is that annoying, little, wining hobbit." The hobbit raised its paw, rather, her hand, bringing my feeling of oneness with the universe to an abrupt halt.

"So, do you think there may be other life forms in that type of galaxy, professor?"

"We will never know. Its three billion light-years away," Dr. Cummings said in a sort of sarcastic, *don't raise your hand again,* manner.

Then the magical staff of the wizard was raised up. "What about worm holes, professor?

Some say, that's a way for, well, aliens to travel those billions of light-years, moving through black holes between three and two dimensional quantum energy, particulate, vibrating folds.

"Wait… Did he say, 'vibrating?'" I tried to keep my thoughts streamlined on the discussion about galaxies. Yet, other gravitational g-forces kept pulling me back.

Dr. Cummings paused before giving his reply. I always called him, "Dr. Cummings." It was more personal to me and matched my crush of a fantasy I had of him. He was tall, dark, handsome, and mysterious. All the sound bites of a "hot guy," with an added encrypted code of

sexuality not of this world. I think thirty-something. But, my hand shook too much to measure any data and read my impassioned celestial compass. He had the most beautiful green eyes and when he spoke, I always became fixated on him with a nature-driven raw intensity even more so than that distant galaxy now before me upon the screen. I tried to imagine what it would be like to be with him, to have his hands move upon me… in some type of theoretical, dimensional goose-bump feed within a *vibrating* fold in time. I found myself slightly parting my pressed legs.

"I'm aware of that theory," Dr. Cummings responded to the wizard, jarring me from my thoughts of wanting him to ravage me, startled, for a brief moment, of him possibly being able to read my mind as he glanced over at me. I quickly pressed my legs back together.

"However, we don't, truly, understand how worm holes interact in relation to black holes in terms of Particulate and String Theories.

Scientists have only begun to explore those types of interstellar dynamics," Dr. Cummings added in an astrophysicist jest with the wizard as he lowered his staff.

The lights came on. Now, that hobbit was staring at me like a pest I couldn't get rid of. "Doesn't she have *thoughts* of her own? Why doesn't she just crawl back into her hobbit hole."

"We will continue this discussion on Thursday. Remember to complete the chapters on time, space continuums," my infatuation glanced over at me with a smile, sending those tingles, those goose-bumps into my own deep time, space continuum. I widened my legs and got up.

Upon exiting the class, while maintaining my composure with my butt cheeks partially exposed, I noticed the wizard coming for me with a bizarre grin. The hallway was crowded, a lot of student *shooting stars* passing by... So, I found it difficult to escape, continuing to orbit.

However, the wizard captured me, there, out in the deep seemingly unexplored part of the hallway amidst, in a mirrored lens envelope many narrowly focused students on their own lives. No one noticed my capture, me cornered in the Twilight Zone-ish part of the hallway in the corner, except one using a telescope through a lens of jealously – that damn little whining hobbit.

"The professor is an idiot..." The wizard spit out some kind of poison of venom, with his arm around me, somehow cast without me even knowing or being aware, backing me further into a black-hole corner.

"Dr. Cummings?" I inserted as more of a statement than a question in an attempt to pull away from the encapsulated orbit and break free of the wizard's gravitational counter-pull directed into his infatuated obsessed black-hole.

"Yes. everyone knows Particulate and String Energy connect three- and two-dimensional worlds through black holes," the wizard cast his spell, trying to lure me further in. But, I was suddenly able to break free, clinging to the strong stare of the hobbit, something I could anchor upon deep out in space.

"Sorry. I'm not aware of that study," I said, attempting to turn away.

"It wasn't a study, rather converse examinations of relative connected theories of space and time, String concepts about curvatures in space..." the wizard twirled his staff in an elliptical manner, as if attempting to wrap me with string by utilizing is String Theory conjecture and dialogue and... it worked. That one got me. I felt his energy pulling me back in becoming bound by his gravitational force. I had just done a paper on String concepts and its relative components between time and space. I thought brilliant, at the time. Somehow, the wizard knew... His spell

was working. He knew something about me that I didn't... He began toying with me as if he just captured a specimen.

"And you are?" I said with a slight gasp, downward turn of my eyes.

The wizard reached out his hand toward me, although I didn't reach back to shake it, wanting to just curl up in my glass jar–the one he had one hand upon while in the other, a dissection scalpel.

"Julius. I'm part of this Hologram we're existing in, demonstrated by, as a matter of course, the mystery of black holes. I'm very interested in..." Julius stared down at my bare exposed legs... toward my crotch, "the structural dynamics of black holes... Hey, I really like your costume. That's a costume, right?" Julius asked, acting like he could disrobe me and dress me while captured underneath his glass with his flowing long blond hair, glistening...

"Of course it's a costume," the hobbit said, finally coming out of her hobbit hole in the corner of the hallway. "Do you think she's really a slut? You know what they say, people dress up for Halloween as what they really would like to become..." she added.

"So, how long have you wanted to be a hobbit?" I asked, trying to shove her back into her hole. Julius laughed. The hobbit, or whatever it was, became angry and stormed off down the hallway. My phone rang. It was Crystal. "Excuse me, Julius," I said, breaking free, moving in the opposite direction as the hobbit down the *opposite* end of the hallway, this position in space.

"Hey, Crystal."

"Hey, girl. Still in your sexy whore outfit?"

"Yes," I responded sarcastically, noticing Julius maintaining a strange stare upon me, watching me as I continued down the long hallway that appeared to become longer with each step.

"It doesn't sound like you're having fun with it," Crystal said.

"You don't know it, but you just saved me... Listen, I really think there was something in that pot..." I began to open up, trying to find a portal to escape Julius's *freaking me out* stare.

"Why do you keep talking about the pot?"

"Okay. I'll tell you. I know this sounds crazy, but I had a fantasy about being with a woman, a zombie… It seemed so…real, like Deja Vu," I said.

"Wow… Really? Well, that's perfect timing. Look. I felt bad about making you go to the library, again. So, I set you up on a date, one of my girlfriends. I told her about you and…"

"Come on, Crystal. I keep telling you, I'm not gay…"

"But, you're having fantasies about being with a woman, right?"

"It was just a fantasy created by your drug laced pot…" I turned away from Julius's far distanced stare from down the hallway.

"I don't think it was from the pot. You're not the only one who observes… the universe."

I turned back around. Julius is heading toward me like a comet, coming close to a planet's atmosphere, dangerously close, something that could wipe out all of my preconceived species of perceptions about life as a I know it and my preconceived sexuality. Quickly, I try to hide under a rock, or something, as a last ditch effort to escape this oncoming weird comet.

"I just thought it might be good for you to, you know…research your feelings within, instead of some distant, strange, weird galaxy…" Crystal rambled on, fading into a distant echo as that *strange, weird comet,* now stood before me.

"Okay. I'll do it," I simply replied to Crystal with Julius established in a domineering manner within my defenseless air space.

"Really?" Crystal responded, with a slight pause as if she was analyzing the encrypted data to my response. "So, I'll confirm?"

"Yes. Tell her I'm very much gay and interested…" I tapped in the Morse "Girl" Code within my response back to her.

"That's great! I'll tell her… She just came out too. I want you to know that I'm so proud of you. You're finally opening up…"

I hung up, slowly lowering my phone, my last shot from a laser gun projection to defend my planet and my interplanetary, "Black Hole." "I missed," I thought as Julius began smiling.

"I don't think you're gay," he said to me, intercepting and crushing my "Girl" Code. "How do you…" I began to ask, pausing, I think telepathically.

"I noticed how you stare at him," he said. "Him?" I thought.

"Yes. Him. The professor," Julius captured me, feeling totally open and vulnerable before him. I had to find a way out, a secret passage kind of way, something… I had to buy time.

"Can I help you, Julius?" I asked, somewhat startled that he just moved even deeper into my air space with his comment a seductive touch on my shoulder.

"I forgot to tell you. There are other closer… entities, you know, that can support life. Zeta Reticuli one and two…" He said, not blinking, maintaining his stare. All I kept thinking was, are they his real eyes? They look different."

"What kind of galaxies are they?" I asked, with a curiosity of what was orbiting within his dark purple appearing eyes, like some distant undiscovered galaxy.

"It's a star system, thirty-eight million light-years away," He said, physically moving closer, now caressing the side of my cheek with his long fingers.

"That's pretty far away," I responded, attempting to take a step back.

"Not really," he added, taking hold of my hand. "The system seems pretty close to me."

Strangely, his gentle grasp of my hand, created a slight gasp from within me that spilled out as quickly I attempted to turn away and cover it with a cough, sliding my hand away…

"I heard, it can be experienced clearly in the Southern Hemisphere," he said, pulling me back toward him.

A deeper gasp. "Sorry, my Southern Hemisphere is closed… to men," I affirmed what he had overheard, finally breaking free and walking away.

"You're really biologically attracted to females?" He asked, catching up to me, walking alongside of me, down the hallway.

"You look nervous. Do I make you nervous?" He asked, trying to re-take hold of my hand. I responded, pulling both of my hands to my chest.

"Maybe we can have lunch. You have to eat… You're human, right?" He stated, smiling, as if I was a control group in one of his experiments. I turned. The strange sunglasses fell out of my backpack. His smile faded as he bent down to pick them up.

"Where did you get these?" He projected in a demanding manner as Dr. Cummings approached.

"Is everything alright, here?" Dr. Cummings asked, giving a hard stare back at Julius as if they had an ongoing disagreement from somewhere else.

"Why, yes. We were just talking about…" I began to say, to calm things down and find separation as Julius finally, finally took a couple steps backward in this brief time and space continuum..

"About space," Julius, respectfully nodded toward me.

"Yes," I blurted out again, adding, "We were just talking about space and… I think I need some. Excuse me," I said, turning away again, so many times turning away, walking back down the hallway, exposed in my philosophical and physical sexy outfit before both observers of men.

"Are you well versed in the laws of attraction, professor?" Julius asked Dr. Cummings. "I just wrote a paper about it, subatomic particles that make up matter, energy, waves, even we are attracted through these kinds of quantum particulate connections," Dr. Cummings responded to Julius as I continued down the hallway, not even looking down at my phone.

"Correct, Professor," Julius said, adding, "You attract what you put out into the universe." "Are you a physics major?" Dr. Cummings asked.

"Right now, I'm majoring in, you could say, biological genetics," Julius responded still watching me, checking out my legs and butt as I walked away, exiting through a door.

I took a breath. I looked down a high stairwell. The man in the peculiar grey suit was far down at the bottom of the stairs… looking up at me. Shocked, feeling stalked, I gasped for the third time, this time much deeper, much more intense. Yet, surprisingly, I found myself walking down the empty stairwell toward him, shaking with each step, as with each step, he took a deep puff of his cigar. Pausing, looking back up. I could hear the stairwell door I just passed through lock. I looked back down. He was still there, the smoke from his cigar, rising upward with his stare toward me. I stumbled, almost falling. So, I took off my boots and placed them gently by the side of a stairs.

Then, I continued on, barefooted, down the winding deep centered stairwell toward him, smiling. Slowly, I removed my short shorts, stepping out of them, tossing them down the stairwell, then my football jersey, number 77, floating down, disappearing in the smoke. At the bottom of the stairs, followed by my panties. I found myself, suddenly, standing completely naked before him…his yellow slanted eyes staring down at me, as if examining me…

Smoke engulfed the hallway…

"Do you mind if I join you?" Startled, I awakened and found myself poised over open books upon a long mahogany table within the university's library. "Ugh. Julius again," I thought as I wondered how I had gotten here and when. I seemed like I traveled through some void in time. "What happened the strange man in the suit? Was I fantasizing again? The pot?"

Julius pulled out a chair and sat down close to me. I glanced down at my phone on the table. No call from Crystal, not yet. Silence. I thought about sending out a distress signal.

"You know, I gave it another look and confirmed what I originally thought," he said. "About black holes?" I replied.

"About you being gay," he said. "My hypothesis and conclusion is that you,.. do like men. Yet, I added another variable, ran it again, and you may in fact also like women. But, I'm okay with that," he added as if I had no choice in the conclusion of his social experiment in which I was his subject. Julius said all of this in a weird, peculiar manner as I looked around the library, nervous, apprehensive, okay- frantic. Only a few people were there, far off sitting at other tables, and a librarian. She was my only anchor of hope, standing behind a large central desk

"I have to go soon," I simply responded to him, staring over at my silent phone. "Ring, come on, ring, a text tone from a scammer, anything, anyone," I thought.

"I only need a few minutes," he said as if he had a plan for me that involved some kind of experiment.

"A few minutes, for what?" I boldly turned toward him, holding back my nervous gasps. "So, what are you studying?" he asked, studying, checking out my bare legs, again.

I pressed them together, placing one hand discreetly over my crotch. "I'm studying black holes," I said, "Possible dimensions of the dynamics of bent time…"

"Ah yes, Black holes," he responded, glancing down at my hand. "I've ran the analytics that may prove they are, truly, pathways between three and two dimensional universes."

"Within dimensions of time?" I asked, flashing back to standing naked before the peculiar man in the suit within the cigar smoke, hovering, as if suspended in time around me.

Julius looks away from my legs, pushes his chair back. "Yes. I believe that there are opposing parallel universes within dimensions of time. But, time can, of course, be defined differently, depending upon the... observer." Julius leaned closer, whispered in my ear...

"A dichotomy of universes?" I asked, suddenly interested, adding with an unforeseen ever so slight echo of a sexual orgasmic gasp, "But... How?"

Julius slid his chair closer. I kept my eyes down at the open book before me on the table. He glanced around the library and began to whisper, placing his arm around me, "When the Big Bang occurred there were particulate explosions in... simultaneously, two directions. Recently, I discovered a mirror universe where time moves backwards, yes, backwards. Well, to those in that universe, it moves forward. We move backward. It's kind of complicated, comes down to the observer, like I said..."

Julius looked around the library again as the few people began to leave. He got closer to me with a softer whisper, softer internal voice. "Don't tell anyone. But, I'm working, right now, on a way to track them. I'm a good tracker." I noticed his eyes turn bright blue... like the sky.

"Am I one of...them?" I asked.

"Of course not," Julius said with a smile, adding, "You're just a biological vessel... they are searching for." He looked down at my legs, again, toward my crotch, placing his hand, now, on the upper part of my thigh–*tapping one of his long fingers upon it.*

"We're closing in a few minutes," the librarian said to us, approaching. "Do you want a security guard to walk you to your car, hon?" she added, looking at me directly.

"I'll make sure she gets safely to where she's supposed to go..." Julius said, closing the book that was open in front of me while giving me an extra tap on the upper inner part of my thigh. The librarian appeared concerned. I remained silent, noticing on the book's cover very strange symbols. The symbols appeared familiar as I stood up. I found myself, again, lost in my fantasy of standing naked before the man with yellow eyes. He reached out his hand toward me – Reptilian. I felt his scaly hands upon my bare breasts... my bottom's cheek... I gasped as he took me, my head arching back my hips pushing forward, my legs wrapped around him…

Suddenly, awakening again, I found myself in real time of the present dimension, walking across a desolate campus with a few light posts, dimly lit, and a couple of students far off in the distance with, of course, Julius, closely following me by my side like my shadow.

"Why are you doing this?" I asked Julius, walking at a fast pace to get away from him. "I just want to make sure you're safe, that's all," Julius responded, adding, "Look. Do you see those flashing lights?" Julius pointed toward lampposts along the sidewalks of the campus–*Flickering in the remnants of my, Girl Morse Code.*

"That's how they communicate, a kind of alien type Morse Code," he explained.

"I was right!" I thought. "Who do you keep talking about?" I asked, looking around at the dark and eerily quiet empty campus, seemingly on another planet.

"Time, the quantum molecular realm, stars, galaxies, streams of energy, we're all part of something bigger and they're a part of it, too," he said, no longer smiling, looking around, as I, staying closely by my side as I headed toward a light–the bus stop.

"They, them… Who? Part of what?" I asked, trying to keep him in his own…space. "Not, who or what. But, how? By Design," he said, mapping out a simple formula. "You see, nothing is random. There are no coincidences. Like us meeting. It's part of a larger equation, a kind of undiscovered mathematics… hidden within envelopes of time.

Shocked. I stopped. "What's the matter?" Julius asked, now, wondering about me. I looked over and saw the man in the peculiar suit, standing by a lamppost, smoking his cigar. Julius looked over, too, but couldn't see him, though sensed someone was there. "Do you see someone?" Julius asked, adding "You see someone, don't you? I know you do."

"It's nothing, no-one. Let's just keep going," I responded, turning away from the man watching me, feeling naked, again, very vulnerable in the persona of the reality I chose to pursue. I just shook my head and moved, quickly, with Julius continuously following. A bus approached us as we made it to the bus stop. I turned back. The man in the suit was gone.

I entered the bus and sat in the back, staring blankly out the window as the bus driver drove us away with Julius watching me, standing at the bus stop. The street's lights flickered… Julius looked down and discovered a key. He reached down to pick it up. Smoke, a cigar was suddenly tossed down at his feet. I realized, later, *my lost key* would eventually open a door to that part of the universe I was searching for…

As I gazed out the windows of the bus, I looked back and saw Julius still standing there. He continued to watch me with the lights of the campuses lamp posts suddenly begin to flicker in synchronic type codes around him. He just nodded with one last touch of his look… Then, suddenly, the man in the peculiar suit, the one I was sexually drawn to, suddenly behind him. The flickering lights increased as if a finale of fireworks.

The man, he put his hand on his shoulder. Julius turned. The lamp post lights went out.

Darkness. I turned away, cradling my thoughts, glancing around the bus, wondering. There was a man sitting in the back, rough looking, like a construction worker. His clothes were covered in soil, yet his boots appeared cleaned, not a mark on them. A woman sat in front of him. She had on funny glasses and her hair didn't look real. She looked over at me, giving me a stern look. I quickly glanced away… wondering.

CHAPTER 3
Captured by the Light

When I get back to our apartment building, later that night, carrying my fantasies in my other purse, I couldn't seem to find my key as I looked through my backpack of reality. I soon realized that Crystal had hurried me so much; I thought, I must have left the key inside the apartment. Nervous and upset, I began imagining long Grey fingers moving all over my naked body, turning me over and placing me on my stomach as another Grey, behind me, arched my neck, straining it, pulling back my hair...

"I can't believe this," I said to myself, shaking my head, more so in reference to my fantasy. As I entered down the hallway of our apartment, I continued to search for my key in my backpack. Feeling frustrated, I couldn't find it as I kept walking with my head down, searching, feeling my way along toward laughter I heard echoing from the other side of our apartment door. Standing before it, still not able to find my key, I decided to knock. The door opened before my hand touched it, finding myself knocking on air...

There, stood Crystal, one arm slumped over the shoulder of a very cute young man, tall, dark hair, brown eyes, with dimples, and, the most important part, who was checking me out, staring at my legs. Ugh. I had forgotten what I was wearing. I looked away as if not noticing.

"She's gay," Crystal said to him, abruptly, noticing his flirtatious look directed toward me, adding, "I'll call you later," with a smile, pushing him out the door past me while pulling me in. Closing the door behind me and locking it, Crystal kept her smile. She was wearing a short tee-shirt with *Believe* on it, nothing else.

Noticing her remaining smile, I said, "He was that good, huh." Crystal nodded as I asked, "And was he coming on to me?"

"Of course he was. You probably had a lot of... people hit on you, today, in that outfit," Crystal responded going over toward a table and opening a drawer.

"Too many. Felt embarrassed, and in a way, very vulnerable. It was like I was a hidden planet and everyone wanted to land on me," I said with somewhat of a slight smile.

"Is that a bad thing?" Crystal asked, searching through the drawer.

"Maybe not for you. But, for me, I like to be in control of those who enter my atmosphere," I replied, tossing my backpack on top of my bed by the telescope and open window, causing the strange metallic sunglasses to fall out.

"Well, that's the thing about releasing one's wild side. You never know what you'll attract..." Crystal noticed the sunglasses. "Were you excited, though, about experiencing..." She went over, slightly pushing me aside, and picked them up. "Alternate realities... Where did you get these? One of your admirers?" She asked.

I took them back, placing them back into my backpack. "I think I'm going to give my wild side a break, for now, wear something that says, *studious astrophysicist student,* tomorrow.

"Why? Are you giving up on saying, *I am a sexy whore.* You're just getting started with your new courageous, intriguing look. Why are you giving up so soon? You, apparently, got a lot of attention. That's what you were searching for, right? Through your introspective telescope." Crystal said, gently touching and moving my telescope toward me. I took hold of it, moving it

back into position. "It wasn't what I envisioned," I said as Crystal turned away and went back over to the opened drawer.

"It never is," Crystal said, resuming her search into the drawer.

"So, when I am supposed to go out on... this date you set me up with?" I blurted out. "Tonight," Crystal, in a matter of fact manner, responded.

"Tonight? Really? Do I have time to get ready? I don't even know what I'm going to wear..."

Crystal looked up and smiled at my outfit. "Why don't you just wear what you have on," she said, adding, "I'm sure she'll like it. She's very excited about meeting you. She's an athlete."

I don't know if I'm ready for all of this. I'm so confused. What if I change my mind and this isn't what I want? Will she understand?" I asked.

"You'll be fine," Crystal stated reassuring me. "You need to stop exploring the universe so much and begin exploring what's inside you... Found it!" Crystal pulled out a bag of pot from the drawer. She rolled a joint, lit it up, and took a couple of puffs. She then opened a large bottle of wine and popped on music as I, apprehensively, sat down on my bed with my legs, once again, pressed together, glancing up at myself in the small mirror. "Who am I?" I thought...

"Let's party and unleash those inner fantasies," she said to me, taking more hits of the joint and a couple slugs of the wine, adding, "Who knows? Maybe your fantasy zombie woman will reappear, again, and become your reality." She reached out the joint toward me, pulling me up off my bed.

"Oh, no," I responded, reluctantly standing up. "More pot? What's in it this time?" "Nothing. Really. Come on. You're date will be here, soon. Let's celebrate your coming out," Crystal said, still reaching out the joint, a Gateway to the Universe to...well, I didn't really know. A Worm Hole? I glanced toward the telescope, pointed out the window...

"My coming out?" I didn't come to that empirical conclusion, yet..." I responded, interrupted by a sudden hard knock, pounding, at the door.

"That's probably her," Crystal said, walking over and flinging open the door. No one was there. She looked up and down the hallway. Empty.

"That's strange," Crystal said to herself. Crystal re-entered the apartment, leaving the apartment door slightly ajar.

"Who was it?" I asked.

"Don't know," she answered, adding, "Probably that nosey neighbor again. You know, the one with weird eyes. It's like she's always watching us or something." Crystal approached me, again, and again reached the joint toward me.

"Take a hit. You know you want to, sista from another universe. Why are you letting your inhibitions kick in, now?" Crystal asked, appealing to that part of me deep within that desired and yearned to explore my sexual fantasies hidden in *another part* of my *East Side Galaxy*.

Not wanting to *suddenly take off and jettison into space,* I responded, "There is absolutely no way, I'm going to smoke any more of your..."

Flash of Interstellar Light… Booming, pulsating rap music. Wall Clock Stopped 1:11 am.

Smoke permeated the room with rap music blasting. Crystal and I were indubitably stoned, totally free of inhibitions with are inner selves bare to the universe. We were dancing and singing, rapping, and then… of course, stripping. My boots went first, then my jean jacket, then

the sheer, white, short shorts… tossing them atop end of the telescope. Crystal wore the metallic sunglasses as I danced, shaking my hips and butt in just my pink thong panty while wearing my straw cowboy hat and small #77 jersey.

"Go, Maria! Shake it, sista!" Crystal chanted along with the music toward me.

I closed my eyes and kept dancing, feeling warmth of a subtle sudden breeze coming in, awakening those tingles up and down my spine from when I saw him, the man with the grey- yellow eyes, feeling his touch upon my cheek…

BRIGHT LIGHTS. Humanlike small figures with smooth grey color skin, enlarged elongated heads, and slanted eyes emerged from the smoke of pot permeating the room. Crystal noticed them first, appearing shocked, fearful, pointing toward them with her mouth agape. "Maria," Crystal struggled to whisper as if frozen in a permeating silence.

My eyes opened in shock. I tried to call out but my screams were silent as they took hold of me, grabbing me from around my waist behind, feeling their long grey fingers around me and the cast out images of their dark slanted eyes… as they pulled me back toward the open window. I couldn't break free as I attempted to scream out louder within the befalling silence as Crystal reached out toward me, seemingly from another dimension as they yanked me with more of a solitude of force out the open window and upward into bright hovering lights. Crystal's cries grew faint as silence grew around me, except for those small echoes of sounds of traffic in the city streets far below…

"Maria!" Crystal's voice grew distant in her dimension, drowned out by the city traffic below while she gazed up in shock, staring out the open window as I was pulled upward by an unknown force, seemingly a reverse gravitational pull, toward a hovering elongated lighted disk. I vanished into a darkened void, feeling coldness upon my skin, tingling bits of less air centered upon me, flowing as sand from a glass and into my lungs, gasping for air within a vacuum of complete silence–and a twirling tunnel of darkness. I found myself floating, moving upward toward an opening, a light, as I was frozen in fear, unable to move, in a horizontal position, face- up, rising… and rising, further and further away from our apartment building in the distance as with the sounds of the city's streets far below. I closed my eyes, as if I had entered a dream, hoping with each struggled breath that I would awaken in my bed and realize it was just a dream.

Crystal, curled up in a fetal position in the corner, appearing catatonic, twirling her hair… remained trapped in icicles of fear, a frozen dimension, with the rap music still sounding out, the smoke escaping out the open window as the music faded, upward toward a star filled sky draped in a befallen stillness… of silence.

Floating in the reticence of darkness, feeling like I was submerged in water, I continued to be elevated in my prone position, my arms outstretched by my side, upward, through an intense crepuscule cyclone of a warped spinning tunnel. Finally, once above the surface, I opened my eyes, took a deep gasp of breath and realized I could breath again as I was lifted up into something that appeared to be some kind of metallic spaceship. The *Greys,* who captured me, quickly, stood me up and hurriedly guided me down a long hallway with unusual purple lights upon the internal metallic walls as other young women, as if in a trance, were being led down another hallway, wearing short robes of white. As they gripped me tighter, pulling me faster down my hallway, a few of the *Greys* appeared to be piloting the ship with several, appearing to be like robots, standing still, aligning the hallway; emotionless, unmoving, without expression, seemingly disinterested in me being led by my arms as their captive, probably one of many, down their futuristic, out of this world, appearing purple haze UFO hallway.

With even stronger grips, they lead me into a large room where there were other humans sitting on metallic benches, seemingly in trances, centered around and above a long, shiny, metallic table. The *Greys* slid off my thong and removed my short jersey, as I eventually stood frightened, motionless, shaking, unable to move, totally naked before the other clothed humans who were smiling. I turned my head, slightly, standing totally nude before the *Greys,* frozen in a type of unyielding fear, not able to fight back or break away although my thoughts wanted to escape, now, this *West Side Story* of the my inner mind's fantasies. Being manipulated, they laid me down on my back upon the cold metallic table as I looked up into bright lights as if I was in an operating room. They then, methodically, proceeded to stretch me out in a wide spread eagle position, tightly binding my wrists and ankles with cold twisted wire that cut into my skin, stretching my arms and legs further out, very wide. One grey spoke to me. But, he didn't use words, just thoughts.

"It will be alright. We have to do this," he said, looking down at me with his large oval shaped black eyes, his scaly grey skin, and his long fingers, one that gently touched and caressed my bare breast, moving it gently, tenderly across my nipple. I glanced away as the sensations of his long fingers caressed my other breast, made me tense while still hoping it was all a dream.

Yet, at that moment it seemed so real as I found myself strapped naked, spread-eagle on my back to this cold metallic table that began to vibrate with electrical type pulses. There I was—surrounded by slanted-black eyed Humanoids, standing above me, totally nude, bound, and vulnerable. They could do anything they wanted to me as they gazed down at me with their long, grey fingers reaching out, touching me in places that made me squirm and intensely tingle within their inhuman caress of a touch. My face convulsed, my legs tightened, and my toes curled. But, I was unable to move nor even scream out. My eyes showed my intense emotions of fearfulness as they widened with one tall grey getting closer, hovering over me… watching, staring.

Closing my eyes, tightly, hoping he would go away, I felt him position himself, climbing a top of me in a mating position. I tensed more in pain, at first, yet felt a sudden rush of shamed exhilaration as he slowly entered me. Gasping, writhing, my heart pounding, I opened my eyes, moaning out in immense sensation and despair. As he went deeper inside of me, I never imagined anything like that before. My entire body convulsed and writhed, exploding in sensations of both ecstasy and revulsion while other humans in the room watched us with programmatic cold looks. Their faces appeared unemotional, unmoving as I gazed back into his eyes. He smiled. I cried.

Then I realized, glancing back into his grey-yellow eyes. It was him, the one I fell for. "It's you," I gasped out, finally able to speak as he vanished… They left me there on the metallic table and cleared the room except for the one grey, who said, "We have to do this." The grey who initially examined me, gently.

"We are doing experiments, cross-breeding. It's part of a mission. You'll understand one day," he said telepathically to me as he undid my the bonds upon my ankles and wrists. Being released, I immediately went into a fetal position, crying, gasping, shaking, not knowing what else they had planned for me. The grey then held up a long metal probe. He pushed me further onto my side and then slid the long, cold, steel probe up into my bottom. "Stay still," he just commanded me. I winced, shutting my eyes one more time, wishing I was somewhere else... He pushed in the probe, deeper, further into my anus. It crushed my thoughts of dignity, feeling his long fingers caress my bare bottom's cheeks and the stares becoming more pronounced from those who watched... I attempted to picture myself in a field, flowers, and a small creek, flowing past thick woods of pronounced silence. Yet, there within them, were these eyes, staring, watching, as I suddenly found myself bare and vulnerable, standing before them... they.

I wanted to cry. But, I was too terrified to do so as the pain became more intense. If was as if they were doing some type of surgical procedure but without any anesthesia. There was no where to drift off and awaken from. I was totally submissive to their power, unable to make even the slightest effort to resist... as from the smoke I saw three of them with surgical masks.

A hand reached out with some kind of needle. They embedded it into the side of my neck.

I felt the sting, the puncture as they measured my feet and hands with a flat long instrument. Turning me over onto my back, they even wrapped it around my breasts, tightening it, with clicking sounds of measurements as they put a thin, shiny, elongated, tube in my mouth, sucking my saliva into it.

They pressed down on my tongue as I felt their scaly, cold skin hands pushing the sides of my cheeks aside. One face got close, his slanted eyes almost touching mine as he caressed my forehead, seemingly attracted to me. I tried to turn away. But, I couldn't. They had me frozen, somehow, paralyzed in a warp of time, unable to scream, unable to shout, unable to turn as they inserted a long cold needle into my vagina...

With a silent scream in my mind–I closed my eyes and cried out!

Sounds of traffic. A loud truck's horn sounded out. The next morning, Crystal awakened, lying near the open window. She slid off the sunglasses.

Looking up, she noticed my pink thong draped upon the end of the telescope. The night was over as the smoke had cleared the room and Crystal, shaking off slight disorientation, arose and went toward the open window. She looked out and up into the sky.

"Maria?" she whispered. She heard a moan. She turned. She saw me in my bed, shaking, clasping upon the Red Rosary beads with the soft sounds of the ticking wall clock, beginning to move again away from 1:11 am.

My body frozen within that moment in time, my eyes opened – *terrified.*

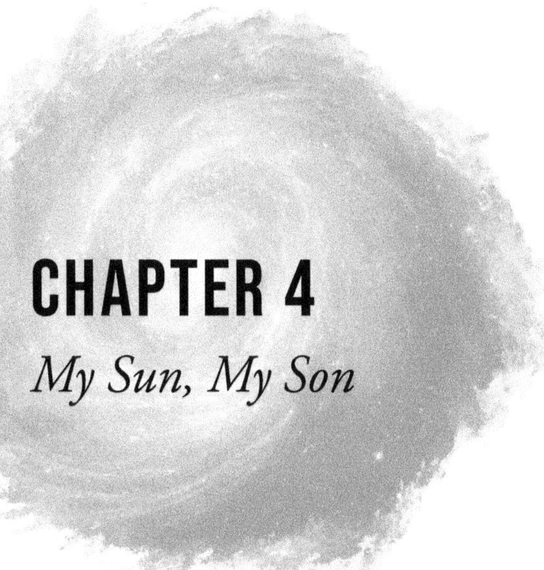

CHAPTER 4

My Sun, My Son

I close my journal, briefly glancing up and out the window at the grey cast mountains on our spanning acreage ranch before me and the bright sunlight. *I glance over to the aquarium, my son's large pet green iguana, still staring at me, watching…* I then look over at two pictures of my sons, Christian, a fighter pilot on active duty in the air force, and… "Hey, don't you have to pick up Brandon? It's almost 2:45," Crystal calls out to me from the doorway, causing me to turn away from the *iguana's stare.*

I jump into my converted Ford-250 pick-up Monster Truck, pop the clutch into gear, and peel away from out Ranch House, down a dirt road, with small stones spurting up from my path. Crystal watches by the front door, as I drive away–LOUD SOUND–GLASS BREAKING. Crystal turns toward my bedroom…

A GREY ALIEN'S hand reaches out and picks up my journal. Crystal opens my bedroom door. A rancher, a middle-aged Hispanic man, Issac, stands by the side of my desk. He appears to be concerned–staring up at the BROKEN WINDOW PANE.

"Must have been birds… or something," he says to himself as Crystal stands in the doorway.

"Can I help you… Issac?" She asks. Startled, Issac turns. Crystal notices my journal in Issac's hands.

"Found this on the floor when I came in. Just putting it back," he says, placing my journal back upon the desk with green unusual triangular scars on his forearm.

"What are you doing in here?" Crystal asks, entering further.

"Sorry. I'm looking for Maria. It's important. Need to talk to her, right away," he says manipulating the conversation toward a sense of urgency.

"She went to get Brandon. Is there something I can help you with?"

"We found something up on the West Ridge. I know Maria keeps a lot of books on that subject in here. So…" Issac says, trying to explain himself.

"So… are you looking for Maria or her books?" Crystal counters, cornering him, as part of her skills of manipulation, toward the pointed edge of my desk.

"Actually, both… Yes, both. We think there is a connection with…" Issac says, looking away and out the window toward the grey mountain range.

"I am sorry, Issac. I don't care to hear anymore about your conspiracy theories. You can tell Maria. She'll be home soon. She believes you. I don't. I don't believe anything you say. You can leave, now. You shouldn't have been here in the first place," Crystal commands him in a superior authoritative manner.

"Yes, ma'am," he says, bowing his head, beginning to leave.

"What do you think broke that glass?" Crystal asks, staring at the window. "Was it you, Issac?" Issac pauses, glances back.

"No, ma'am. Not sure what it was," Issac gives one more bow and leaves.

Crystal moves toward my desk. She looks down at my closed journal– STRANGE AZTEC ANCIENT SYMBOLS ON ITS COVER.

I push harder down on the accelerator of my monster truck, speeding across the desert, reflecting upon my sons, similar, but so different. My son, Brandon, is an apparent genius, sweet and introverted, diagnosed with Asperger's, yet, a perfect student from the perspective of a neutral observer… Straight A's, never in any kind of trouble… Yet, like all kids… As I drive toward those grey cast mountains. My phone rings… I answer.

"Hello," I say with apprehension, noticing the number is from Brandon's school. "Ms. Rivera?"

"Yes," I reply, trying to figure out who it is…

"This is Mr. DeGenova. Sorry to call like this, but I wanted to let you know, Brandon got into a little bit of trouble today…" I pop my clutch into full gear as the grey cast mountains suddenly appear red, listening to Mr. DeGenova's monotone, yet, seemingly caring voice…

Earlier in the day, Brandon sits in History class, staring at the girl of his dreams–Brandi, an exotic beautiful young woman with long flowing blonde hair and mesmerizing green eyes sitting at a desk a couple of rows ahead of him. Brandon has an I-Pad, cell phone, and strange laptop on his desk before him before him along with other electronic devices. Brandi briefly turns back to Brandon when strangely half of her face, with the illuminated whiteboard with the lights off in the front of the classroom, momentarily, appears to to be reptilian-like.

A teacher from PERU, Mr. Quispe, points to an image of Aztec Paintings on the large illuminated whiteboard screen. The images are that of Elongated Headed ancient Aztecs on remnants of the wall of a pyramid. "This pyramid is very close to where I used to live. As you can see, Aztec culture evolved into find art in which these specific paintings gave a story about Aztec life at that time…"

Tommy, Brandon's best friend, leans over to him, breaking him out of his inter- galactic infatuated trance, staring at Brandi. "They had really weird heads," Tommy says, barely above a whisper.

"Oh, yeah," Brandon replies, not noticing.

The intercom sounds to change classes. As Brandi gathers up her things, Brandon continues to stare at her as she gets up and exits the classroom.

"Come on, bro," Tommy says to Brandon. "Let's go."

Brandon puts his books in his pack back along with his technology devices and follows Tommy out into the school's hallway. Tommy opens up his locker next to a symbol of the school's mascot–an alien with an elongated head and slanted eyes as Brandon watched Brandi reach up into her locker, brushing back–as if in slow motion–her long blonde hair, briefly glancing back at him with unusually beautiful green-eyes.

"Dude, why don't you just ask her out, already? The proms coming up," Tommy says to him as he remains frozen by her beauty as if tugging forcibly at his heart within some distant twirling dimension in time.

"She's got a boyfriend. Probably going with him," Brandon dismisses the opportunity while at the same *time* fixated on her long flowing hair.

"So, what? Doesn't hurt to ask, right? I mean, what could happen? Tommy says in a counter motion response, refusing to be sucked into a swirling *Black Hole of Doubt*. Brandon continues to stare infatuatedly at her fixing her hair while gazing into a small mirror inside her locker. "You're right. I'm going in…" Brandon says, moving toward his target.

Tommy pats him on the back and nods his head. "Roger that… Spoken like a true fighter pilot… Your brother would be proud," he adds. Brandon gives a thumbs-up sign as he maneuvers his winged courage toward Brandi, cautiously looking for a place to land and ask her out…

Brandi finishes putting on bright colored red lipstick, tosses back her long blonde hair and begins to close her locker. She gasps, somewhat startled. Brandon stands before her, frozen–gazing into her mesmerizing, unusually beautiful, captivating green eyes.

"Hi… Brandi," Brandon stutters.

"Oh, hi Brandon. What's up?" Brandi asks. "Are you alright? You look like you want to ask me something," Brandi adds, noticing Brandon becoming suddenly nervous and withdrawn. Brandon looks back over at Tommy. Tommy gives Brandon an affirmative nod and thumbs-up.

"I was wondering, well… If you would like to go to the prom with me," Brandon says… Hesitantly, Brandi takes out her phone and hands it to Brandon. She apprehensively looks around. "Quick. Punch in your number," she says to him.

Seemingly from out of nowhere, Brandi's locker is slammed shut by her boyfriend, Rocco, a very large well built football player, wearing a football jersey–#77.

"What are you doing with my girl, dude," Rocco says, getting into Brandon's face as Brandon shies away from Brandi.

Brandon lowers his head and replies, "*Nothing*. We were just talking." Brandon hands Brandi back her phone, turns, and attempts to walk away.

"Hey… Where're you going? You hit on my girl like that and then think you can just walk away?" Rocco cals out, moving toward Brandon as he pauses and turns back. Brandon gets between them, pushing her hands up into Rocco's chest.

"Rocco, just calm down," Brandi pleads.

Students in the hallway begin to notice Rocco confronting Brandon. They move toward them, encircling them, from both ends of the hallway. Rocco turns back toward Brandi.

"You're going with me, to the prom, right? I mean, you're my girl…" Rocco says over to her, standing in silence with an appearance of contempt. She turns away. Rocco, becoming more angry, turns back toward Brandon.

"I'm going to kick your advanced placement, gifted and talented ass," Rock threatens. "I don't need this drama, now…" Brandi calls out, throwing up her hands and disappearing down the hallway toward a UFO model spaceship by the trophy case at the end of the school hallway.

With Brandi gone, Rocco shoves Brandon to the floor. The large group of students tighten the circle around them as Tommy attempts to break through the crowd. Brandon suddenly gets up and tackles Rocco. Rocco appears shaken, surprised at Brandon's strength. Brandon and Rocco begin fighting on the floor. Teachers push their way through as other students begin fighting, too. Sounds of an alarm. School SRO Officers rush to the scene…

Casting aside the images of mountain ranges, now, behind me, I enter Red Rock High School and head down a hallway toward the assistant principal's office, not even remembering the drive across the desert. When I enter the office, I see Brandon sitting on a bench, holding a ice pack over his eye. He looks up at me.

"Mom," he says. I just shake my head. Dismissively, I look away. Mr. DeGenova greets me and guides me into his private office. Glancing back, I notice Brandon attempting to listen by the door. I push it partially closed and sit down across the desk from Mr. DeGenova.

"Thank you for coming in, Ms. Rivera. I'll be direct. Brandon is going to have to do an external suspension for fighting and… creating a riot, pending a board hearing."

Brandon gasps, peering in the partially cracked open door.

"Creating a riot? Really? And a board hearing? He's never been in any kind of trouble before," I plead.

"He incited a riot between other groups of students. He was that… spark that created it all. A couple of our teachers, also, got seriously hurt. As I told you on the phone…"

"But, don't you think this is a bit extreme? I mean, what's going to happen to those other students?" I ask, becoming very defensive and now, upset.

"I can't discuss other students, just yours. All of this is in our new zero tolerance policy.

You can access it on our school's website," Mr. DeGenova says going through his desk. "I can't believe this," I respond, blurting out, "How long?"

"I'll notify you once we find out from our board solicitor the exact time lines for the due process in situations like this," Mr. DeGenova replies, matter a factly, and yet, sympathetically. He shuts one of his desk's drawers and looks up at me, directly in my eyes. I notice a tinge of yellow in his which suddenly fades.

"Did you consider what we previously discussed?" He asks in a sympathetic tone. "That accelerated program at Princeton?" I reply, both of us knowing.

"Yes. As we discussed in our previous meeting, Brandon's taken all of or advanced courses and he attained a perfect score on the SAT's I just don't see what else we can offer him, here. It might be good, too, for him to experience another educational setting where he can get a fresh start," Mr. DeGenova says with an increasing compassionate, understanding look of concern, causing my look of concern to increase about Brandon's future.

"Mr DeGenova, Brandon is doing well with academics. We both know that. But, I'm also concerned about his social and emotional growth, as well. I mean, look at why we are meeting. He fought over a girl and now he might have to have a board hearing for creating a riot? He apparently is struggling his feelings, now. Can you imagine him trying to figure out his… emotions, at Princeton University?"

"Good point," Mr. DeGenova says as his phone rings. He answers it. "Tell them, I'll be right there."

"Sorry. I have a meeting," he says to me. Getting up, he politely escorts me out of his office, "We'll provide work, projects, on-line assignments while he's out on suspension. If lightening strikes, I might be able to find him a tutor. But, tutors are hard to come by these days, especially for subjects like physics and the higher-level courses that Brandon is taking… But, you never know.k I may be able to dig up someone from somewhere…" His voice seem to echo.

Alongside Brandon, closely by my side, toward my Monster Truck in the school's parking lot, spanning the white lines, Brandon asks, "Mom…Can I drive?"

"Really? You're asking me that, now, after what you've done? No. Absolutely not. No one, I mean, no one drives my truck," I snip back, adding, "Look, just don't say anything."

"But, mom, it wasn't my fault."

I pause, taking a breath, and turn toward my son, as if starring down the sun, unblinking. "Didn't I say, not to say anything? I saw what happened. You could have just walked away.

You're so grounded. No video games, no phone, no T.V. nothing."

"But, he put his hands on me first…" Brandon attempts to plead his case.

"And what did you do after that?" I push back as he did literally. Brandon remains silent. "Exactly. You're better than this," I add, continuing onward toward my secret refuge, my truck.

As I take hold of the wheel, getting in with Brandon jumping into the passenger's side, I say to him, as a mother trying to teach her child to crawl for the first time, "I keep telling you, you're special. Don't you understand, yet? I can't believe you acted that way. All over some girl," I frustratingly state, accompanied by the loud engine of my truck, a mother's roar, starting up.

"She's not just some girl…She's different," Brandon attempts to explain and defend her. "And so are you…" I add, shoving my truck prematurely into gear, not knowing where I want to take him in the conversation or the road. "Your brother never gave me problems like this," I add, as if strapping him into his seatbelt, speeding away out of the school's parking lot.

Students watch us from the school windows. Brandon becomes embarrassed, silent as he looks up and sees his girl, Brandi, looking down at him through the sun reflected image of glass.

Riding home, across the vast desert, even emptier with no conversation, I notice Brandon staring, quietly, out the window of *his glass* toward those same gray mountain ranges with a look. I can see he is wondering about who he is and, more importantly, who he will become. I had that same look as a child, in the jungles of Peru with my father, years before going to NYU… *"But, you never know. I may be able to dig up someone from somewhere…" Mr. DeGenova echoes.*

Deep in the jungles of Peru at the side of an archeological expedition, exploring an ancient Aztec dig site, as a child, I approached my father, a lead UN research scientist after his service in the air force, flying missions during the first Iraq War. As I approached him, standing within a small hut before a table full of artifacts, he had something in his hand that he was examining with a large magnifying glass. "This is fascinating, Jacob" he said to one of the other subordinate researchers. "Alas, poor Yorick, I knew him…" he added with me standing next to him, looking up at what he held in his hand. It was some kind of… *peculiar elongated skulls.*

"Why do you think it's shaped like that?" Jacob, a thin, short young man with gold wire rimmed glasses, asked.

"Could be just a deformity, or rather, from some kind of Aztec ritual. They did strange rituals back then," my father, as a teacher, answered. My father took a closer look at the skull, fissures appearing like a strange exotic map.

"Strange. These fissures in the cranium are much different than ours," my father said, adding, "Probably just an unique deformity," he added, noticing and smiling down at me as I continued looking up at him. With my admiring look, with respect, he carefully placed the skull down next to other ancient Aztec artifacts as other researchers entered the hut, carrying several elongated skulls. "We found more of them," one researcher said. My father looked toward Jacob, appearing alarmed, his gold rim glasses sliding down to the end of his nose.

"Take us to where you found them," my father directed. I began to follow. "Stay here," my father said to me, leading the other researchers swiftly out of the hut, leaving me to gaze at the elongated skull and the other artifacts. This is the moment, as a child, I began to wonder about the universe. It was this moment that propelled me toward my interest in astrophysics and the passionate curiosity to search for other worlds like the ones, that grew later, within myself... A large part of my childhood, subsequently, became exploring, taking risks, wanting to discover and understand the deepest parts of space, the forbidden, and the unknown. Little did I know that yearning for discovery would lead me to wearing a sexy cheerleader outfit and what lay ahead, that fateful night which would echo before me for years to come. *I may be able to dig up someone from somewhere...*" Mr. DeGenova voice echoed again amidst my memories...

The researchers, carrying these elongated skulls, led my father and Jacob to the entrance of the dig site, far down a narrow slope, at the forefront of a small tunnel. I disobeyed my father, my sister's genes, and followed, of course, discretely from behind, not wanting to miss out on this important discovery of *elongated skull people* living in a deep, mysterious tunnel. So, I followed, ducking in and out of shadows, close enough to hear them talk, yet, without being noticed and I didn't need any kind of advanced stealth technologies to do so, other than being, well, a kid, the kind built on resiliency and "nothing is impossible," attitude. Then, another strange voice echoed among my thoughts, "With God, All

Things are Possible." Where did that come from? I shook my head and focused on driving across the desert, remembering, just remembering…

My father and Jacob stood before the deep dark tunnel, gazing apprehensively into it.

One researcher pointed into the tunnel and said, "We found all of them in there."

My father began examining the tunnel's structure of its entrance- STRANGE FIGH- LIKE SYMBOLS – THE SAME SYMBOLS ON THE BOOK AT NYU'S LIBRAR, the ones I noticed on the table in front of me with that wizard caressing my bare leg underneath the table. "What do you think those symbols mean?" Jacob asked my father, adding, "They don't appear like other Aztec writings I've encountered."

"This was once a road, Jacob," my father answered.

"A road? Underground?" Jacob asked, confused, pushing up his glasses.

"It wasn't always underground, Jacob. These symbols, they're similar to ones they discovered over in England," my father said, taking a closer look at the symbols around the entrance of the tunnel, running his hand gently over them.

"See. They're aligned in similar patterns. In England, from images captured by satellites, they appear to mark elaborate road systems. Do you see how these ovals, intersect?"

I zoomed in on the symbols, momentarily, slipping on a rock. I ducked back down. They briefly turned. They turned back toward the symbols.

"Why would Ancient Aztecs need such a complex road system? And why over in England would there be…" Jacob began to ask.

"They're all over the world, Jacob. We can go into this tunnel to find out, the why," my father said, turning abruptly toward me. "Maria, you can come with us, too."

"Damn. I was caught. But, somehow I knew, he knew. My father always knew. So, I just smiled, coming out of the shadows, moving toward a dark mysterious tunnel of my memories.

My thoughts crossed with my abduction experience of being lifted up into a tunnel of light. My hand reached over and held Brandon's. He turned from the window, looked at me, smiled and said, "It will be alright, mom. I'll figure it out." The touch of my hand reaching out from my most horrific moment, illuminated a connection between me and my son. I nodded back at him, looked ahead out into the desert, finishing my memory connected with that dark tunnel.

Using flashlights, all the researchers, Jacob, my father, and me entered this ancient tunnel, not knowing what lay ahead. I would find out later in life that each search, each exploration, each discovery would bring with it a sense of a revelation within oneself.

"What else would we find in there, besides strange looking skulls?" I thought, following my father closely from behind.

"Stay close," my father reaffirmed to me, reaching back and taking me by the hand as we entered into the darkness of a void, feeling cold, the flashlights illuminated less—more and more.

"According to astrophysicists, Grey Aliens, Zeta Reticulan, account for many alien abductions. They possess humanlike small bodies, smooth grey-colored skin, and elongated heads," Brandon says, staring back out toward the mountain ranges in front of us, getting closer, breaking me from my thoughts of the *dark tunnels* even *the illuminated one* of the past.

Surprised, I ask, "Why did you all of a sudden think of that?" It was if he was a part of my memories, somehow, connected with him from my mind, my memories.

"Don't know. It just came to me," Brandon replied, adding, "I guess because we're studying about elongated heads that were discovered in Peru."

"How did you…" I began to ask but fell into silence, thinking within my current reality. "Coincidence. But, what about what Einstein said? Never mind. Maybe I was too hard on him. That girl is very cute and he seems to really like her, and didn't I teach him not to back down to bullies?" I took a breath and retrieved my center, again, all those yoga classes, lessening the grip on the large wheel of my monster truck.

"Hey, your brother requested a leave to come see us?" I spoke in a softer tone, hoping to get him to turn away from staring at his own reflection upon the glass.

"Really?" He asks, excitedly, "That's great!"

"Yes. He said he's coming back for a few days," I add, seeing his enthusiasm grow with a sense of renewed confidence. Feeling in a better place, Brandon begins to tell me everything that happened at school with the girl, Brandi… As he does, I realize how much he likes her, causing him to become something he's not, or rather, something he should become to be… *Sound of a text message on Brandon's phone.*

"Who's that?" I ask. "Christian. He sent me a video of him flying his new fighter jet." "Wow. That's perfect timing" I smile, close to the mountain range and our home as Brandon plays his brother's video, flying over the Baltic Red Sea...

Sounds of Fighter Jets. Two fighter jet pilots maneuver their jets above the Baltic Red Sea, flying over the USS Nimetz-Delta Aircraft Carrier, during routine combat flight exercises. Christian Rivera, Brandon's older brother, turns up music in his cockpit from the Woodstock Music Festival, 1969, a *Summer of Love.*

"Nothing compares to the music of the 60's. Can you imagine what it was like, back then? Half a million covering on a farm at Woodstock..." Christian says over the radio to the other pilot, Jessy in the jet by the side of his...

"You don't have to go back that far to find great music," Jessy says.

"True. But, there's just something with that time period I find intriguing," Christian responded. "Like I'm caught in some kind of time warp, through music..."

"Look out!" Jessy cries out, seeing a fast moving UFO pass before them.

Christian, suddenly, sees the UFO appear out of the clouds, heading right for him. He quickly turns his jet. The UFO circles back around both jets–making 90-Degree turns. "Do you see that, bro? What do you think it is?" Jessy asks.

"Don't know. It's acting crazy. How's it making turns, like that? Christian replied, adding, "Lets Rock "N" Roll–maneuvering his jet in an attempt to follow the UFO at a high speed while recording it on his phone. "Damn, that thing's moving fast. Haven't seen anything like it before..." "Do you think it's one of our's," Jessy says, turning his jet to follow, too.

"We don't have anything that can move that fast. No. It's something else..."

Suddenly, the UFO appears by the side of Christian's jet, seemingly appearing as an arising haze of blue. There is a window... Christian stares at it. He sees an alien, large head, slanted black eyes. He appears to smile at Christian, who appears shocked, confused, as he pulls back the throttle of his jet and watches the UFO disappear into a Bright Colored Horizon.

I push down on *the throttle* of the accelerator of my monster truck, riding across the desert toward the rising gray mountains seemingly touching the sky. Brandon turns to me to show the video of Christian's flight operation, over the Baltic Sea.

"Look what Christian sent me," Brandon says, excited. He was always excited to hear from his brother. He admired him so. Knowing this, I hesitantly let Brandon show me, in a way to get him to focus on the present, not the misgivings of the mistakes of the past, nor the unknowns of the future, just him and me, driving across the desert toward those grey mountains. We begin to watch the video… of the UFO… AUP…

At the bottom of the valley of the West Ridge, wind blows sand over top spanning large circles embedded in the soil, appearing like symbols. A scarred arm reaches out for my journal on the desk with the same symbols upon its cover…

Crystal stands by a stockade fence, staring blankly toward two horses trotting about the enclosure. She reflects upon that night… curled up beneath our apartment window, staring up and out the window toward a star-filled sky of unanswered questions. She turns as we approach from the distance… *"Sometimes, to find the future, you have to go back into the past," my father once said to us…* Driving toward our family ranch house, I felt I was driving toward a past…

I think of my father and all that he taught me. He taught me at a very young age how to ride a horse, a small white pony named Lucy. She was so gentle. When my father placed me atop of her, it was as if she was helping me get on too and once upon her, she moved cautiously with each step as my father walked alongside of me, holding me on. But, even at a very young age, I knew my father couldn't hold onto me forever. At one point, we both knew that he would have to let go. But, I still remember him guiding me, feeling as if he is still by my side, talking to me in those quiet moments when no one else is around. I love quiet moments. As I glance over at Brandon, I felt bad how I reacted. I wanted to apologize. But, I knew this wasn't the place or time. I knew, like my father, that I had to help guide Brandon in making the right decisions and not reacting with his emotions. He has such a brilliant mind and a great heart. I think to myself, I hope the world will treat him kindly. It's strange–I never taught him to ride…

CHAPTER 5

The Mysterious West Ridge

As we drive up to the ranch house, the gate is open to the stockade fence for the horses. Two stallions, one brown and one white. I park my monster-truck off to the side, away from the that big white oak tree to ensure the birds don't get it, again, causing my shiny black coating to peel. Glancing over at Brandon without a word, he jumps out after I park and walks in silence up the steps of the porch and into the house as I double check to make sure the engine is not on. For some reason, although having a lot of technology, my truck had a mind of its own, and like those stallions, would often want to escape and run off. I approach the gate to close it…

I put the rope over the two posts as I had done for at least a thousand times since we moved back here. Almost a couple decades later, I came back to Arizona on the family farm with my sister, Crystal. She's a doctor, now. However, although living in a high-end condo, she often comes by. We've remained very close over the years. She never married. Yet, I did, an Air Force Captain. He went missing about eight–no nine-months ago without a trace. The search by the Air Force and FBI still continues. But, I don't hold onto much hope. I diverted all my energy, for my sanity, toward taking care of my two sons, Christian, an Air Force pilot, my stepson, stationed on an aircraft carrier oversees, and my own child, Brandon–my biological son, although I am unsure of the true father, and no, I just don't believe in DNA tests, especially with what I experienced in that lab, the cold table. Yet, Brandon, he's brilliant, too smart at times. He has a big heart, a wondrous, compassionate spirit and soul, and is very passionate about learning about new discoveries of the universe, especially the possibility of life on other planets, which is coincidental.

Most of all, though, he adores his older brother, Christian and wants to be so much like him. Strangely, even though Brandon's brilliant, he struggles as a senior in high school with his emotions, his social/emotional growth. He has a lot of friends and, now, likes that beautiful particular girl at school, Brandi. I noticed, watching the video, there is something special about her. However, Brandon lacks the confidence and does not know how to approach her to make "that connection" similar to my situations, growing up, with regard to intimate relationships because of what happened "that night," or at least, that's what I believe…

Two of the horses come up to me. I pat their manes as the one white one, Silver, stands off in the distance, watching the mountains as if he knew something. I turn and see Crystal coming out of the house, passing Brandon along the way.

"Hey, what's up with Brandon?" She asks. He looks upset as he passes her, head down, without a word.

"What's up with Brandon?" She says to me while glancing at the two horses with apprehension.

"He just got into a little of trouble at school," I respond as I notice the horses becoming agitated, especially Silver, whinnying, kicking and bucking.

"What's a matter with them?" Crystal says, taking a step back.

"Don't know. Something is spooking them. Never have seen them act like this before.

Come on, lets take them for a ride, maybe it will help them calm down."

"Oh, no. You know I don't like horses. Remember the last time?" Crystal says, taking another step back."

"Come on. You'll be fine…" I take off the rope and open the gate. I go over and place the saddles on both Silver and Crystal's horse, Blaze.

"Are you coming or what?" I ask as I mount Silver, pulling back on the reigns.

Crystal hesitantly walks through the stockade fence and approaches Blaze. He bucks a little as Crystal attempts to mount him.

"I told you, I don't like horses," Crystal says, struggling to do the mount, finally getting atop of him, clinging to the reigns.

"Why can't we just take your truck?" Crystal adds.

"Because where we're going, even a monster truck can't take us there. But, these horses, with their spirit, we can…" I respond with a guiding nod and smile.

"Where are we going?" Crystal asks.

"The West Ridge," I simply respond as Crystal abruptly pulls back on the reigns. "What's the matter?" I ask, noticing a frightened appearance on her face, blending with that of the horse.

"The West Ridge… Issac told me to tell you he found something up there." I pause too, pulling back. "What else did he say?"

"Just that he needed to talk to you. He was snooping around in your room like he was looking for something."

"I'll have a talk with him. There must have been a good reason," I respond, wondering, more like, sensing something big was about to occur.

We ride off to the West Ridge of our ranch, what Silver was mysteriously gazing toward from within the stockade fence that many of us place around us in our lives, not knowing we have the power to step beyond… Several strange things had occurred up there on that ridge over time, especially recently.

"Maria!" Crystal cries out as Blaze, suddenly takes off. "Blaze! Calm down! Please stop!" Crystal attempts to pull back on the reigns of Blaze, trying to control him as he gallops toward an unseen destiny. Blaze always acted different with Crystal. It was as if he enjoyed teasing her by bucking, twisting, and galloping as she cries out. I just had to gently kick Silver into a faster gallop, leading toward *The Mysterious West Ridge… in a way, traveling back into the past crossing with the future…*

Twenty-years later–after the incident of being abducted by those grey alien beings, now I sit upon thoroughbred horses on the West Ridge of our family ranch in Sedona, Arizona, gazing out across the valley toward a *New Day* with an optimistic sun, brighting shining in the distance, peeking behind the mountain range.

You can't capture the sunlight of your soul, something whispers to me with a slight forked echo emanating from my cerebellum enthralled at the beauty, at the unusual colors above the mountains. A storm had just passed through the night and a soft breeze within a captures frame of time, momentarily and gently, blows back our hair as we sit upon the horses, gazing down into the West Ridge Valley below.

Turning toward me, pausing in a taken breath, Crystal says just above a whisper, "So do you remember anything about what happened that night?"

Twenty-years later after the incident, Crystal and I sit upon thoroughbred horses on the West Ridge of our family farm in Sedona, Arizona, gazing out across the valley toward a sunrise.

I remain silent in my trance, glancing out...

"You do, don't you," Crystal whispers to me, yet to herself, somehow knowing. Crystal pulls back on her reigns, moving closer to me upon Silver as I glance back at her with a why are you getting closer to me kind of look.,

"You remember. You finally remember," she adds.

I tighten, pulling back on the reigns of Silver, beginning to turn away.

"It's interesting, isn't it..." Crystal maneuvers Blaze with the inflection of her voice as seemingly a processed Ancient Oracle, emerging out of character, staring blankly out to the mountain ridge, and then, to the valley below.

"I think the answers are down there," she says, crossing with my same thoughts. "What?" I ask in PAUSE just to confirm.

"That light above the mountains seem to be like your memory, hiding for years, and yet, for whatever reason, upon this moment— shining through..."

"You think my awakening memories of that nigh are somehow connected to that light beyond the mountains?" I ask, confirming my own thought.

"Wasn't it Einstein, who said, 'There are no coincidences?'" Crystal responds with a smile, adding, "I'm starting to remember too..."

I remain silent to that line from long ago. She was right, or Einstein was. Realizing we were being guided toward something, the West Ridge, it was then, I finally let completely go of the reigns, gazing out toward the bright sun, rising higher above the mountain range, as the colors of my own universe appear to move with a feeling of a force of a moving planet in a perpetual elliptical motion through space... I begin to remember... as we ride back down, into that distant valley below with the echoes of 2001 swirling around us upon the encircling mountains.

We both notice, at the same time, LARGE CIRCULAR MARKS IN THE SOIL. We pause. Look. Wonder… The sensation comes back from that time, long ago…

"What do you think they are?" Crystal asks.

"Don't know. Let's keep going, take a closer look," I say with another kick, pulling back on the reigns of Silver and continuing to lead the way down into the deep valley below. We rode as if entering an awakening light, a new day, with the circular marks becoming more and more prominent in our minds, crossing with other lights, humanoids, and scream.

I flash back to being bound by my wrists and ankles, their slanted black eyes looking down at me, their long fingers… touching me… I close my eyes and let Silver lead the way. Somehow, he knew too, gently guiding me through my past and into my future… the answers trapped within the remnants of my soul.

Once in the valley, before the strange circular marks, we begin to get down off our horses. Yet, Crystal clings to Blaze, not wanting to let go, before she finally does. I bend down and lean over touching one marking, a few inches deep…

We have to do this, echoes in my mind, touching the mark, feeling him, his power over me… "Do you think kids did this? Crystal asks, pushing the memory away.

"Maria…" She snaps, bringing me back.

"Oh, what?" I find myself in the future, the present of my soul.

"Do you think kids did this? With motorcycles or something? Crystal asks with a proposed answer.

"Kids wouldn't know how to do this," I respond, getting up, being lifted from the metallic table. I brush off the dirt of my hands and look up at a group of ranchers, riding horses, approaching us.

"Maybe they know," Crystal says, shading her eyes from the bright sun, beaming down upon us as if beneath a spotlight on a stage, as the shadows of the riders got closer.

"Do you ever wonder why he came here?" Crystal asks.

"Who? Issac?" I respond with an elevated high pitch in my tone. "Yes," Crystal responds in a deep monotone. "Isaac."

"Don't really know. He just showed up on my doorstep, one day, saying he was looking for work. So…"

"So, you made him your lead rancher. Just because he showed up when you needed someone."

"I thought, at the time, it was too coincidental, like Einstein. So, I hired him."

"And you don't think that's strange? Just showing up on your doorstep? Wasn't he a priest or something? That's what he said, right?"

"A lot of people have career changes," I reply in an *En garde* fashion.

"A teacher to an attorney, that's a career change. A priest to a rancher, that's just weird." "So is a whore to a doctor," I respond with a winning thrust of my saber.

"Touché," Crystal says with a nod and smile.

"Well, he's here, now, and he's been a godsend since my husband disappeared." "Why do you always call, Roger, you're husband. Why don't you just say, Roger?" "Because I don't like to give things names," I respond.

"Why?"

"Why? Because… because it hurts too much…"

The ranchers ride up before us, kicking up dust from the soil, their horses appearing aggressive coming to an abrupt halt.

In a brighter sunlight than the bedroom, Issac, an attractive Hispanic man, somewhat short, yet well built, seemingly in his mid-forties, with a large white cowboy hat, gets off first, followed by the other rugged group of ranchers, wearing brown leather, cowboy boots and hats. Issac tips his hat at Maria and Crystal. He squats down and touches the markings. I flash back to being touched by long grey fingers, my breasts, inner linings of my body orifices. I wince.

Crystal notices.

"This is the second time in the past two weeks," Issac says with the other ranchers surrounding him.

"What do you think they're from?" I ask, glancing over at Crystal appearing frightened, like that night.

"They appear to be from something that landed here," Issac says, looking up at me. "Landed?" I ask, bewildered and confused, curling up within me.

"Like a spaceship?" Crystal asks, appearing more frightened. Issac does not respond, examining the embedded circles with more scrutiny.

"I saw on Facebook, there have been a lot of strange things happening on ranches close to us, right Crystal?" I add.

Isaac rises. "I don't know what's happening on other ranches. But, ours, it seems like they picked this location for some reason. There are no coincidences."

"Says the cowboy, Einstein," Crystal blurts out. "They? Who are they?"

Issac looks at me and responds, "Don't worry. I'll make sure our ranch is protected." "From what?" Crystal asks, adding, "And our ranch? It's your ranch, now, Issac?" "It's all of our ranch, Crystal. Everyone who lives here," I thrust my saber again with more of a determination.

"Oh, come on, Maria. Wake up. He's playing you… And who are 'They?'" "You know the 'They.' Don't you, Ms. Crystal," Issac says with somewhat of a threatening tone, as if he knew…

Crystal, suddenly, became silent, frozen, imagining being trapped beneath that open window, in fear of what will happen next, clinging to the metallic sunglasses as Issac and the other ranchers get onto their horses.

"We'll go out to the East Ridge, ma'am," and see if there is anything there," Isaac says directly to me, ignoring Crystal, pulling forcibly on the reigns of his horse, kicking with a determination the back of his horse, riding off with the other ranchers following.

"Let's go back. I want to check on Brandon," I say to Crystal, staring out toward the past.

She nods, gets onto Blaze without a complaint and leads the way back as I follow atop Silver, glancing back at the strange, mysterious, circles…

2001. "Maria!" The Light. The Slanted Black Eyes… I reach out and take hold of the Red Rosary Beads. Clutching them to my chest, close to my heart, I begin to pray, transforming into a child with my father standing over me. He gently and quietly leans down with me upon my bed and says…

"My dear, daughter. You are so precious. I wish you the most beautiful life in which all your dreams come true. You're adventures will be miraculous and your path will be bright. For you are a child of God. His Light within you. This Light will be passed onto your son, a son with much brilliance and courage. Many will seek him, for his special gifts… Stay close to God, my child… For He is the Way, the Truth, The Light."

As we ride back across the desert, Crystal has a look of both concern and bewilderment. I too wonder what's going on, if *they, for some reason,* had somehow come back for me. Would I have to go through that again? I glanced over at Crystal, sharing the same look, the same fear from years ago, that may have just caught up to us...

Blaze all of a sudden takes off, bucking and galloping, into a full run... as Crystal clings to him, clasping frighteningly to the reigns.

"Maria!" Crystal cries out...

"Maria!" Crystal cries out, in the past, beneath the open window as I am abducted up into the tunnel of time, into the hovering UFO...

I pat my horse, Silver. "Come on Silver," I say gently to him as he gallops into a trot following Blaze and Crystal.

"Never again!" Crystal cries out, adding in a shout, "I am so done with horses!"

CHAPTER 6
A Jungle, a Symbol, a Family Secret

A United Nations research team, deep within Peru's jungle, discover a tunnel near an ancient pyramid. Dr. Samuel Drago, an astrophysicist, leading the expedition, stands next to a research scientist, Dr. Julius Baker, nickname, *The Wizard*, wearing a straw cowboy hat. They both notice the strange symbols around the entrance of the tunnel with several other researchers. They cautiously begin to examine the symbols. Dr. Drago is very tall, lean, about fifty-years old.

"Be careful," Dr. Drago says to them, adding, "We have to move cautiously. It doesn't look like anyone has been in this tunnel for quite a while. Judging by those symbols, it looks like they date back to... possibly the fifteenth century."

"You know what amazes me, Dr. Drago? Julius asks.

"What's that, Julius?" Dr Drago replies, gazing further into the dark tunnel. "How can an astrophysicist know so much about anthropology?"

"Because everything is connected, Julius," Dr. Drago says, moving into the tunnel, adding, "What amazes me about you, is how an anthropologist can know so much about astrophysics. Is that what you studied in college?"

"Actually, Biological Genetics," Julius replies following Dr. Drago and others into the tunnel. They light their flashlights. The tunnel is cold, damp, with various insects crawling about. A small stream flows beneath their feet as small reptiles jump in an out of the view of the light.

"How far are we going in?" Julius asks, expressing some concern. "As far as we can, until..." Dr. Drago replies.

"Until what..." Julius asks, wondering.

Dr. Drago shines his flashlight on the wall. He sees a skull, partially protruding out. "Do you think this is some kind of burial site?" Julius asks, handing Dr. Drago a small shovel. Dr. Drago takes it and carefully digs out the skull.

"Wow. Look at that," Julius says with the other researchers appearing amazed. The skull is elongated. Dr. Drago puts it into a small black backpack.

"Are we going to look for others?" Julius asks, looking down the long tunnel.

"Do you want to?" Dr. Drago says with a smile as they hear something moving, making strange humming sounds about fifty-yards away from them deep within the tunnel.

"I'm good," Julius says, turning back with others nodding.

"That's what I thought. I concur. This will help us figure out what this tunnel is or, rather, was. Besides, this might be a burial site. If so, we'll get this skull back here where it belongs after we figure everything out," Dr. Drago says, leading them back out of the tunnel. "We have the pictures of the symbols, the skull, the coordinates in relation to the pyramid. That's more than enough to get a foothold on what this all means," Dr. Drago explains as they exit the tunnel.

Dr. Drago stands facing Julius. "Biological Genetics?"

Julius tips his straw cowboy hat. "Yes. I explored a lot of... biology back in college, even created my own experiment. "If you call making love to a woman an experiment," Julius lets out a strange bellowed laugh. "Yes, yes... I experienced a lot of Biology."

"Good. Then you can hold onto this," *Dr. Drago* replies, handing him the backpack... Dr. Drago turns back. He notices something inside the hole where they retrieved the skull. He takes out small shovel, reaches in, digs, digs some more, and takes it out. It's a small piece of a strange blue-gallic metal, shining, like a flickering morse code of lights, reflecting amidst the crossing–conflicting flashlights. He lifts it up, examines it, examines it some more.

"What's that?" Julius asks.

"I'm not sure," Dr. Drago says, entranced as if in a spell, a mystical bond within his eyes and the shiny strange small piece of metal. He lowers it, breaks free of this trance, and hands it to Julius. "By the way, I'm heading out in a couple of days."

"To another excavation?" Julius asks, gripping the backpack and small piece of metal. "No. Teaching. I decided to go back to teaching," Dr. Drago replies with a smile, adding,

"Maybe our paths will cross again, Julius…"

Upstairs in his bedroom, Brandon is lying on his bed reading a book about astrophysics and theories about aliens. He glances over at an old poster on his wall of *The X-Files,* "The Truth is Out there," and begins to read aloud, "According to astrophysicists, *Draconian Aliens,* from the Alpha Draconis Star system, possess a reptilian-like appearances, green eyes, and ShapeShift to control humans within shadow governments…"

Suddenly, he hears a car pull up to the front of the Family Farmhouse. He puts the book down on his bed, gets up, and goes to the window. He smiles. Christian gets out, carrying a suitcase and a black backpack. Brandon bursts out through the porch screen door to greet him.

"Mom! He's here!" Brandon cries out to me.

"Hey, it's good to see you, bro," Christian replies with a hug. "Heard you got into a little bit of trouble, bro. Hope she's worth it."

I exit the house and approach Christian. "I can't believe it. You're finally home," I say, kissing Christian on his cheek.

"Just for a couple of weeks, mom. That's all they would give me."

Brandon picks up the small suitcase and black backpack. He gestures to Christian, lifting up the heavy suitcase. "Wow. What do you have in this?"

"Something for you, bro," Christian says, putting his arm around me and smiling at Brandon. Issac approaches upon his horse accompanied by the group of other ranchers.

"Is that the ranch hand you were telling me about?" Christian asks, appearing concerned. "Yes. His name is Issac. He's been a big help to me, a Godsend," I reply.

"Ma'am, we checked out the East Ridge. No signs of what occurred on the West Side.

But, we did find…" Issac begins to say atop his horse before me and my sons.

"Thanks, Issac. We can discuss it later. Oh, this is my other son I was telling you about, Christian."

Issac tips his cowboy hat. "Heard you are in the Navy." "Air Force. Did you serve?" Christian replies.

"Yes, for several years," Issac says, pulling back on his reigns, steadying his horse, encircled by the other ranchers.

"Issac used to be a priest," I say, taking hold of Christian's hand.

"A priest? Why did you…" Christian begins to say, appearing confused.

"Stop being a priest?" Issac interrupts, adding, "Well, you never stop being a priest."

Issac and the other ranchers turn and ride away.

"He seems strange, mom," Christian says, squeezing my hand. I lift up his hand and kiss it. "I know. But, you'll get used to him. Let's go inside. I have a surprise for you."

"Let's open what you got me, bro," Brandon says, lifting up the suitcase again. "Okay. Let's do it," Christian replies walking with them toward the house. Before he enters, he gives one quick last turn toward the ranchers riding away toward a mountain with an unusually red-cast sky.

I lead Christian further into the ranch house as Brandon carries the suitcase and backpack upstairs and into his bedroom. Christian pauses and looks into the dining room–"Welcome Back, Christian," sign hangs across the dining room table next to an old grandfather's clock. "Welcome home, son," I say to him. Upon the dining room table are several plates and before them, several empty chairs around the dining room table with a white-webbed tablecloth. Two unlit candles within gold candlesticks are at both ends of the table along with an array of food.

"Looks like you're expecting a lot of people," Christian says, appearing perplexed. "It's just us, me, you, Brandon, Crystal, and oh, Issac," I respond.

"Issac? He's part of the family, now?" Christian asks.

Brandon, standing at the top of the stairs, calls down to him. "Hey Christian! Can you show me what you got me?"

"Sure. Coming…" Christian responds, turning toward his mother. "You have to be careful, mom, with Issac. I've learned, things often aren't what they appear to be."

"Says my son, top of his class at the Air Force Academy. So, what did you get Brandon?" "What's he's always wanted. According to Aunt Crystal, you used to search the stars, too, a while back. Why did you give up…"

"I packed that… part of me away a long time ago. Too many stars, too many galaxies. No. I'm fine, right here, I his orbit with my two sons. I turn and walk away into the kitchen. Christian goes upstairs, sliding his hand up the guardrail, brushing off cobwebs along the way, glancing at pictures upon the wall of him and Brandon growing up together. He pauses at one pic, of Brandon before technological instruments inside what looks like an aircraft.

Christian stands at the doorway of Brandon's bedroom. "So, can I open it, now?" Brandon asks. Christian gives an affirmative nod. Branding flings open the suitcase and empties it onto the floor–*Disassembled Parts of a Large Telescope.*

"Wow! You remembered…" Brandon calls out, examining the parts upon the floor.

"Of course I did, bro. I'll always have your back," Christian says, entering into Brandon's bedroom, standing beside him.

Christian's phone rings–He answers it, turning and walking away from Brandon assembling his large telescope.

Christian speaks quietly into his phone. "But, aren't there any other units nearby that can… Yes, ma'am. I understand. I'll report immediately." Christian puts away his phone. He turns back toward the Brandon. The telescope is completely assembled, pointed out the open window atop a wide, complex tripod.

"Amazing. That was fast, genius little brother," Christian says.

"This is so great. There's supposed to be a Super Full Moon, appearing soon. We can watch it, together." Christian remains silent, appearing upset. "Is everything alright?"

"Sorry. I have to head back to base, catch a flight to my unit from there," Christian says. "But, you just go here," Brandon says, turning away from his telescope.

"I know. Orders. You'll find out, how it all works, someday, bro. Just don't give up searching the stars for who you are…" Christian says, touching the telescope and picking up his black backpack….

Brandon walks alongside Christian, carrying his backpack, toward an awaiting car with a soldier as a driver, getting out and opening the back car side door for Christian. Noticing Christian leaving, I quickly exit the house and run toward Christian.

"Where are you going? You"re leaving without saying Goodbye? What happened?" "Sorry, mom. I was planning on staying. But, duty calls."

I tightly hug Christian as another car approaches. Brandon notices first, then Christian and me. "I wonder who that is?" Brandon says as I release the hug, accepting him leaving.

The car pulls up behind Christian's. The back door opens. Dr. Drago gets out. He walks up and places his black backpack down next to Christian and stares at him in the eyes.

"And you are…" Christian asks.

Dr. Drago turns toward me. "I am Brandon's tutor. I just arrived in town. So, I thought I'd swing by real quick and introduce myself. Hope that's alright. I am sure Mr. DeGenova notified you…" Dr. Drago says, extending his hand toward me. I hesitantly take and shake it.

"Yes. Of course. Sorry. Brandon's saying, goodbye to his brother, right now. But, please, come in," I reply. Dr. Drago reaches back down and picks up the black backpack. He glances back at Christian as I lead him toward our ranch house. Christian appears concerned as he watches me open the door for Dr. Drago, entering our home with me, as if obediently, following. Christian shakes his head and turns his focus back to Brandon.

"Remember to keep your focus on the stars… I'll be back soon…" Christian says, getting into the back seat with the soldier holding the door for him. The soldier gets into the front seat and drives away with his arm out the car window. As Brandon watches them drive away, in a strange prism of a purple light, briefly, the soldier's hand appears *reptilian*.

Standing in the foray of the ranch house, Dr. Drago notices the set dinner table and the "Welcome Home" sign. "I hope I'm not interrupting…" Dr. Drago says to me.

"Not at all," I reply, wiping away a tear, adding, "Its actually good timing. Now, that my son has left, we have an open seat. That's the challenges of being in the military, right? You never when your duty will call… You look familiar. Have we met?" I ask, gathering myself.

"Maybe in one of my… other lives," Dr. Drago responds with me, suddenly, feeling his presence. "You've had other lives?" I ask, my voice quivering a bit, being strangely drawn to his eyes, moving closer to him. He reaches up and gently touches my cheek with a downward cast of my eyes, not knowing how to react to a tingle down my spine with his touch.

"In a professional sense, yes…" He says, pulling his hand away with my rising look. "I get moved around a lot," he adds. "But, I always enjoy what I do… the new adventures," he gives me a nod and a wink.

Brandon enters and looks suspiciously at Dr. Drago. Brandon, cautiously, hands him the black backpack. "Thank you for the handoff. Must have been distracted," Dr. Drago says to him. Brandon stares at him in silence.

"Brandon, this is your new tutor. Mister…" "Doctor. Dr. Drago. Nice to meet you, Brandon."

"I don't need a tutor," Brandon says, abruptly walking by him and up the stairs. "I am sorry, Dr. Drago. Since his brother had to leave, suddenly, he a bit upset."

"I understand. If you want, I can go up and talk to him. I have a good rapport with gifted and talented students." Brandon pauses at the top of the steps to listen.

"Are you a teacher at the school," I ask wondering where he's from.

"I am, now. Just got hired. I'm an astrophysicist though by trade. Enjoy studying physics, astronomy… of sorts," Dr. Drago replies, staring up the staircase. "I am fascinated by the stars."

Brandon shakes his head and walks into his room as Crystal enters the dining room from the Kitchen, overhearing Dr. Drago. "Astronomy, Really? That's amazing," Crystal says with a flirtatious glance and a turn of her hips, right leg in front, left leg back.

"Hi Crystal. I didn't know you were here," I say, noticing her look, the one I've seen, a thousand times before.

"Just came in… through the galactic back door," she responds, adding, "I'm fascinated with the stars, too, and the amazing concepts of astronomy."

"Astronomy is amazing… if you have the right instructor," Dr. Drago responds with a smile in which I see a momentarily yellow tint in his eyes, making me feel concern.

"This is my sister, Crystal. She's a pediatrician. She's staying with us a while. On a Sabbatical. Just broke up with her…

Crystal moves in closer, cutting me off. "Maria. Please. You don't have to reveal all of my… GPS Coordinates," she says, standing next to Dr. Drago, gazing up at him.

"I don't need any kind of GPS. I'm very well versed in particulate collisions and inert forces to come to my own conclusions about underlying… unique positions, " Dr. Drago says, staring into Crystal's eyes, as she appears enthralled, frozen in his returned look, something I've never seen in her before…

Crystal awakens, seemingly from a momentary glance. "Unique… positions? What kind of… positions?" She asks with a wide smile as I roll my eyes.

"Those positions that break away and then… suddenly, powerfully attract and come back," he says, glancing over at me, catching me in a slight nervous gasp.

"So, you don't use any kind of GPS to find your way around. Then how did you find us?" I ask, gaining a sense of bewilderment.

"Looks like another stranger just showed up on your doorstep, Maria," Crystal laughs. "There are various ways to tap into… multi-type-dimensional forces, utilizing time loops from, let's say, within co-existing, vibrating parallel universes," Crystal gasps as he answers.

Gathering her breaths, Crystal replies, "Wow. That's coincidental. Maria is an expert on parallel universes. Aren't you, sista from another universe. Remember?"

"Do you?" I respond to Crystal, picturing her huddled beneath the open window in fear. "I believe, Dr. Drago is just teasing us, using his vast knowledge of astrophysics to…"

"He's teasing us, alright," Crystal says with a flip of her hair, going into the dining room.

Dr. Drago and I follow. "You can sit where you want, Dr. Drago," I say to him.

Brandon, suddenly, appears at the foot of the stairs, looking at us in the dining room.

"Ah, the Prodigal Son returns," Dr. Drago says with a smile and nod, turning, gripping his hand upon one of the empty chairs before the table.

"Two dimensions of time would make travel, time travel of possible. Then time could turn, looping back on itself, like Mr. Drago, said," Brandon says entering the dining room.

"Dr. Drago," Crystal adds.

"Dr. Drago," Brandon acknowledges, adding, "What do you have to do to get a Doctorate Degree? A lot to research?"

"It's a lot of work. Research is involved, also, studying various theories and empirical data, conclusions, publications… Trying to quantify and theorize as to what's real and unreal with regard to the world around us.

Basically, much like what I do now," Dr. Drago says, releasing his grip upon the empty chair. "Are you going to join us, Brandon?"

Brandon nods. I appear pleased. I feel like Dr. Drago has gained Brandon's respect and made a connection with him in which, other than that girl, others could not.

"Well, let's focus on this dimension, for now, and all have a seat. Shall we?" I gesture toward the empty chairs around the table. Everyone begins to take a seat, leaving one empty chair open.

The front door opens. Issac enters. His clothes are soiled, as he appears dirty and worn.

His cowboy hat is off and clutched in his hands. He gazes at us, immediately noticing Dr. Drago. "Issac, this is Brandon's new tutor, Dr. Drago," I say to Issac.

"Issac's my lead rancher," I say to Dr. Drago, staring more deeply toward Issac.

"I know what you are," Dr. Drago says telepathically to Issac as Issac appears shocked.

Dr. Drago turns away. Crystal, still appearing infatuated with Dr. Drago, continues her stare upon him as they sit down next to each other. Issac, hesitantly, enters the dining room. He glances up at the "Welcome Home" sign and places his cowboy hat down on a small table by the table.

"Welcome home," Issac says, adding, "For Christian?"

"Actually, in a way, for all of us now," I blurt out, hoping to make everyone feel welcome and at ease.

"That's a very nice way of putting it," Dr. Drago says with a smile and stare at Issac. "Welcome Home, Issac," Dr. Drago says, adding, "I am sure you had a hard day in the fields."

I sit down at the head of the table as Brandon sits down beside Dr. Drago on the other side of Crystal and Issac takes place on the other side of the table directly across from Dr. Drago.

"This seems lopsided," Brandon says, rising and going to the other side of the table next to Issac.

"Very good, Brandon. You balanced the… equation," Dr. Drago says with a nod. "Well, thank you for coming, everyone," I say, looking around the table.

"It still seems strange having a Welcome Back dinner for someone, who's not even, here, right?" Crystal says lighting each candle.

"Yes. But, don't be surprised what the… human spirit can do. You just need a little faith.

Right, Brandon?" Issac says to him. Brandon nods. I smile.

"Says the rancher," Dr. Drago adds. "That's one theological though. Some people call it, faith. I call it science."

"Dr. Drago is an astrophysicist," I exclaim, "One of his lives. Right, Dr. Drago?"

Dr. Drago is startled as Crystal pops open a bottle of wine. She begins filling her glass to the brim, before her. I glance at her the international stare for stop. In the air, she brushes it aside.

"Wine?" She offers Dr. Drago a glass.

"No, thank you," I don't drink, he responds.

"You don't drink wine," Issac speaks telepathically to Dr. Drago.

"Of course not. You know what I drink," Dr. Drago snaps back telepathically.

Sensing tension, I say, "Brandon, honey, why don't you say grace?" I am hoping Brandon just goes with it, to try to shift the mood, although unheard, into a more gentile kind of setting.

"Grace? We never say, grace," Brandon responds as a teenager in those honest moments. "It's okay. I'll say it," Issac calls out, turning from Dr. Drago's look, and bowing his head as Crystal takes another shot of wine. Everyone bows their heads except for Dr. Drago as Issac begins saying, grace. "Father, thank you for this food and our family before you, Lord. Please guid us toward values of strength, fortitude, and grace to overcome challenges in this universe that may come our way…"

We begin passing food around the table and eating as daylight turns to night. There are a few moments of silence then Dr. Drago says, while stabbing at a piece of meat on his plate, "Our family, Issac? How long have you've been a… ranch hand? I mean, where are you originally from?"

"I've been stationed in many places… in this amazing universe," Issac says not looking at Dr. Drago, continuing to eat.

"Issac used to be a priest, in…" I begin to add. "The Universal Church," Issac says, looking at me.

"That's coincidental. I was once a pastor of a… Church of God," says.

"That's really strange. Two men of the clergy, sitting right here, among us. Who would have thought," Crystal says, appearing to becoming intoxicated. "Didn't Benjamin Franklin say, 'Coincidences are just God's way of remaining anonymous?'"

"That was Einstein," Brandon cuts in.

"So, what church are you a part of, Dr. Drago?" I ask. Dr. Drago gives an antagonistic stare toward Issac. "Not Issac's," Dr. Drago responds in a direct manner.

Issac smiles, wipes his lips with a napkin, and pauses eating, "I understand, now. Why don't you just come out and tell everyone where you're from, doctor?"

"Do you know each other?" I ask surprised. "Our paths have crossed…" Issac begins to say.

"In other lives," Dr. Drago says with a smile, adding, " My most recent station was in Peru, more precisely, the jungles of Peru, a part of an archeological exploration for the government.

"And did you come across anything…" Issac asks.

"Interesting? Yes. You would like the jungles of Peru, Issac. There are a lot of fascinating species in the Amazon… exotic plants, animal pieces, and fascinating unknown remains.

Issac appears concerned as he responds, "I've always been interested in the Ancient Aztecs, their culture."

"I am sure, your church has been interested," Dr. Drago says, reaching over and taking a sip of Crystal's wine. "In the Ancient Aztecs. Do you know there are many passages and tunnels around their ancient pyramids that have never been explored? I wonder what lies within them." Dr. Drago finishes Crystal's glass of wine, sneers at Issac.

"We're learning about the Ancient Aztecs in history class," Brandon says, adding, "They had really weird heads." Issac reaches over to the table and puts his cowboy hat back on.

"Are you leaving, Issac?" I ask.

"Not yet," he responds, adding, "Just getting ready." "For what?" Crystal asks, refilling her glass.

"I don't mean to be so direct. But, shouldn't you be at some church or something, Isaac?

May I ask, what is your divine driven assignment here with these fine folks?" Dr. Drago says. Issac appears to become more upset. "My apologies. Too much digging. Spent a lot of time in those tunnels, lately, searching for answers," Dr. Drago volleys.

"So, you're an astrophysicist digging around in tunnels," Issac says, tipping his hat.

"I am a teacher, now. But, I guess you can say, as in your case of being a priest, I'm still an astrophysicist.

"Then why would be in a tunnel? Shouldn't you be looking up?" Issac asks.

"Ah, yes. I should be. Shouldn't I," Dr. Dragon responds with a hardening look upon his face, adding, "But, you'd be surprised as to what you can find beneath the surface that can connect one with the stars of the universe. I'd be very interested in hearing your viewpoint, sometime."

"About?" Issac asks.

"About faith versus science, the composition of the universe from your church's perspective, of course," Dr. Drago jabs.

"About?" Issac asks.

"About faith versus science, the composition of the universe… from you church's perspective," Dr.Drago replies.

"I think they're both connected. There is no, versus," Brandon jumps in. "Faith is within science. Everything from matter, energy, Dark Matter, Dark Energy, time, warps in space, even life on other planets."

"Other planets? Are we going to start talking about aliens again?" Crystal laughs out, slamming down on the table her empty glass.

"They recently found nitrates near the center of the Milky Way. Nitrates are needed for the composition of RNA, the building block of life. That can possibly mean life could have evolved on other earth-like planets," Brandon says with a new found sense of confidence.

"According to the Book of Enoch, Nephilim, so called, Fallen Angels, have been here on earth for a couple thousand years. There are many accounts of them… forcing themselves upon women to…" Issac says, staring at Dr. Drago along with a deep gasp from Crystal, reaching over for her empty glass.

"Whoo," Crystal says, clasping upon the glass. "I wonder what it's like to be with a Nephilim. Maria, what do you think?"

"That's it," I cry out. "Enough," I say, glancing at Dr. Drago. "Enough," I whisper in a softer tone to his look, a steady stream of purple tint, deep within his eyes. "Please," I end.

Issac returns an antagonistic stare toward Dr. Drago. They both nod.

"Sorry. I shouldn't have gone down this, this tunnel of the past," Crystal says, nodding toward me. "I agree with Maria. I thought we decided not to discuss this conspiracy theory about aliens, anymore. I haven't even heard about the ones called, Nephilim. If they really exist, wouldn't we see them on the news or something?"

"Just because you can't see something, doesn't mean it doesn't exist. We're only in one dimension in time. There are nine other dimensions in our own universe, alone, maybe more, the fourth being time, the seventh being a window to other worlds to possibly more universes," Brandon chimes in, unaware of the conversation at hand, thinking beyond the boundaries of the lattice table cloth and aunt Crystal's clanging glass against others with each hoist of her wine.

"Very good, Brandon," Dr. Drago says to him. "The invisible world; multi-levels of energy and quantum matter, encircling levels of dimensions within orbs of time."

"But, how do dimensions intersect with orbs of time? I don't understand. Don't they have their own relative…time? Brandon asks.

"I have to stop drinking so much wine," Crystal says, adding, "I have no idea what they're talking about, now."

"There are many things… people don't understand, Brandon, and the more they learn, the more they realize how much they don't know about her true design of the realm of our universe," Dr. Drago says.

"Like Versica Piscis. Right, doctor?" Issac asks.

"Versica Piscis? I've never heard of it," I say as a strange force just awakened the dormant astrophysicist side of myself.

"It's the belief, mom, or rather a theory that the universe emerged for the purpose of a Single Consciousness, maybe God… in order to be able to experience itself in many different ways, thus making reality a type of simulation for the single realm, consciousness to experience itself through its creation by becoming the observer, watcher of its own consciousness…"

"Wow. You know about this stuff?" I ask Brandon being totally caught off guard. "Philosophy class. Right before gym," Brandon answers, adding, "I forgot to tell you. I did fifty chin-ups."

"That's great," I respond.

"How did we go from Versica Piscis to chin ups?" Crystal laughs, adding, "So, what's this consciousness you're talking about Brandon?"

"Behind every single point of view, throughout the universe, there is a Consciousness at rest, "I AM" and a Consciousness at play, "What can I become. Exodus 8:14," Issac replies.

"Ah, Exodus. I love reading the Bible. So, what do you believe you can be, Brandon?

That's your first lesson, envisioning what you can become and, more importantly, what you are, you're I AM…" Dr. Drago says.

"Mom, why didn't you ever take me to church?" Brandon asks. "Yes, Maria. Why?" Crystal adds, knowing.

Dr. Dragon smiles back at Brandon and says, "Perhaps your mother brings you to God in different ways, Brandon."

"I started to… but…" I begin to say.

" A priest turned rancher, and you know about, the Consciousness of the Universe…

That's perplexing to me, Issac," Dr. Drago turns his attention toward him.

"I thought we were going to stay in our own dimension. You three seem to be communicating on an entirely different level of… consciousness," Crystal blurts out.

"Very good, Crystal," I say with somewhat of a twisted smile. Crystal raises her wine glass to me.

"It's the wine," She responds.

"Does your kind have a conscious awareness, doctor? A soul?" Issac asks. "Your kind?" Crystal follows.

"It seems you understand me much more than a common rancher would, and for that matter, a common priest. Did you learn about Versica Piscis in the seminary before your gym class, Issac?" Dr. Drago asks.

"Issac like to watch the documentary about Ancient Aliens," Brandon says. "Is it true, Issac. You like documentaries about aliens?" Dr. Drago asks.

"Issac told me how Dark Matter and Dark Energy are always combatting each other. But, Dark Matter seems to always find a way to win. It may consist of a black hole, a burned out star, or gamma rays that just need a trigger to reignite it's energy," Brandon adds.

Dr. Drago appears confused and responds, "I didn't realize, Dark Matter has that much power, since matter and energy appear to… be manipulated within dimensional warps of space and time? Ancient Aliens, Issac?"

"What's Dark Matter? Where is it?" Crystal asks.

"It makes up eighty-five percent of the composition of the universe," I say, coming out of my self cloaked persona from years ago.

"No," Dr. Drago says, making me wonder. "Yes," Issac says.

"Yes?" Dr. Drago asks.

"Yes. I like watching Ancient Aliens," Issac says to Dr. Drago with a smile. "Touché Are you part of Dark Matter or Dark Energy, Issac?" Dr. Drago asks telepathically.

"You said it. You know what I am," Issac responds telepathically to Dr. Drago.

"I am sorry. But, I must excuse myself. I want to check out what we saw out on the West Ridge early in the morning. Good night," Issac turns and says to me.

"Good night, Issac," I respond, adding, "By the way, I am still interested in having a follow-up discussion about what we found up there. We might have to put in some security technology, cameras, lights, things like that."

"Yes ma'am," Issac responds, adjusting his cowboy hat, leaving. "I must also excuse myself," Dr. Drago says, appearing curious.

'Before you go, maybe Brandon would like to show you his new telescope. It could possibly be a tool to be incorporated into his lessons, perhaps?" I say as Dr. Drago pauses and glances over at the grandfather clock. "Sure, I have a little bit of time," he says with a smile. "In a linear sort of way," he adds to Brandon. "Shall we?"

Brandon nods. They get up from the table and Brandon leads Dr. Drago up the staircase.

Crystal immediately turns toward me. "What was that all about?"

"Dr. Drago and Issac?" I ask, adding, "Probably just bantering, like two roosters in a henhouse, showing off how much they each know about the universe. You know how men can get, sometimes.

"I thought your expertise was with women. I see that bin re opening," Crystal says, teasing me... lifting her glass.

"I think you've had too much wine," I reply to her, getting up from the table.

"Okay, I'll just say it. I don't think it's a good idea for you to allow Dr. Drago to tutor your son," Crystal says, emptying the rest of the wine from the bottle into her glass.

"Why?" I ask, clearing the table.

"Because I think you should find out more about him. Why do you always let whoever shows up on your doorstep immediately come into your life? Why didn't you just let him leave?"

"Because he made a connection with Brandon. Maybe he can help him," I say, glancing at the staircase.

"He also made some kind of connection with Issac," Crystal says, attempting to rise, swaying a bit, steadying herself on a chair. "He doesn't seem like a teacher, more like some kind of spy or something."

"Mr. DeGenova wouldn't send me a spy to tutor Brandon," I turn toward the kitchen. "Did you notice how he kept staring at me?" Crystal says, releasing her grip on the chair. "Actually, you were staring at him. I think Brandon can learn a lot from him, right now, and I don't want to be alone with what he's going through, emotionally," I walk away toward the kitchen, carrying the plates. I enter the kitchen and place the plates into the sink.

"A rancher who was once a priest, a tutor who acts like a spy, you sure know how to attract them!" Crystal cries out, echoing through the kitchen door.

I push the kitchen door open and confront Crystal, sitting back down on one of the chairs. "I really don't care what those men are or are not. My primary focus is on Brandon, right now.

You wouldn't understand," I say, beginning to clear more food from the table.

"Why? Because I never had any kids to raise? Because you to two kids to raise, one from someone you don't know and one of your husbands?" Crystal says with a jab.

I drop the plates. "What do you mean, one with someone I don't know?" "You know."

"Know what?"

"That you don't know," Crystal says, appearing upset.

I pick back up the plates. "I thought we agreed to never talk about it," I say, turning my eyes away from Crystal's direct, angered stare.

"I think what matters is that Brandon and Christian are both my sons, no matter who is the father, right?" I say, strongly, accepting where I am. "Do you still think about…"

"My miscarriage? There isn't a day that goes by that I don't think about my child… I think it was a girl," Crystal says, putting down her glass.

"Are you sure you were pregnant?" I ask, sitting down next to her.

"I keep telling you," Crystal says affirming, "I vomited for three days. I felt it. I am sure.

And I know this sounds crazy. But, somehow, I think my child is still alive, somewhere." "Alright. Let's just agree again not to bring up anything about that night. I put it all away back into that bin, years ago. It's sealed tight."

"Well, maybe it's time for you to finally unseal it…" Crystal says, pushing her glass toward me as our hands touch, clasping together… embracing in a tight hug.

In his bedroom, Brandon is looking through his telescope, out his bedroom window with Dr. Drago standing behind him. "May I give it a try?" Dr. Drago asks. Brandon moves aside, takes a step back, as Dr. Drago takes his turn, looking through the telescope.

"Nothing is better than an instrument to explore universal mysteries," Dr. Drago says, focusing in on a light emanating from Issac's small apartment above a barn as Brandon text messages Tommy.

Brandon–*Hey, is there a new science teacher at school*

Tommy–*Am I allowed to be talking to u*

Brandon–*Come on, bro*

Tommy–*No new teachers, bro. Y*

Brandon–*See what u can find out. Name–Drago. Can u pick up my work 2*

Tommy–*Will do*–Brandon looks up from his phone. Dr. Drago is watching him.

"Is everything alright?" Dr. Drago asks. Brandon doesn't respond, lowering his phone and putting it into his pocket. Dr. Drago smiles and adds, "There aren't many students who asked to participate in Princeton's advanced program… Let me punch in my number." Brandon hesitantly hands him his phone. "You know about Princeton?" Brandon responds, surprised.

"In my… position, I get moved around a lot. One minute I am in the jungles of Peru, the next, I am showing a brilliant and gifted student how to… navigate the universe. Dr. Drago turns back and adjusts the telescope–gazing into it, seemingly with more determination. He points it upward, higher toward the sky while handing back Brandon his phone.

"The amazing thing about telescopes are that everyone points it at their particular favorite shooting star… Take a look."

Brandon leans in to the telescope–A SHOOTING STAR. Brandon's phone rings–BRANDI. Brandon hesitates to answer, backing away from he telescope. Missed Call–Brandi. Brandon appears upset. Dr. Drago notices.

"It's okay. I have a feeling your… star will come back into your orbit again, soon. Faith, right? Like Issac said. Or is it quantum mechanics, possibly a combination of both.." Dr. Drago says, looking back into the telescope. "The thing about physics and life is that one never can predict what will happen. Life often unravels in surprising and miraculous ways, connecting everything in a mesmerizing sequence of events… I see something different in you, Brandon, a gift of creation. Do you know anything about the Metatron Cube? Dr. Drago glances toward him.

"Yes. It contains thirteen circles and straight lines, all geometrical platonic shapes identified within…"

"Creation," Dr. Drago stands upward, facing Brandon. "Yes, the Flower of Life. You know, some believe that it's named after a guardian Archangel of heavenly secrets of the universe," Dr. Drago glances out the window, back toward Issac's Apartment. "Tonight has been very informative for me on many levels. Thank you, Brandon."

Dr. Drago leaves with a nod and pat on Brandon's shoulder. After Dr. Drago exits, closing the bedroom door, Brandon suddenly notices a light shining from Issac's apartment toward him. Illuminated symbols, from this light, mysteriously appear upon his bedroom door. He goes over and places his hands upon them–Oval Symbols–Thirteen Lines/ Circles. The telescope turns…

Issac's apartment atop the barn, a candle is lit before a small altar with a Cross. He kneels down to pray. His apartment is adorned like a small chapel, religious paintings, candles, statues. The door of his apartment opens–casting a shadow through the light of the candle–Dr. Drago, with his black backpack over his shoulder stands in the doorway.

"What are you doing here?" Issac asks, turning and arising.

"I have the same question for you," Dr. Drago says, adding, "May I come in?" Issac nods. "Well, this is interesting," Dr. Drago says, entering, gazing at all the religious paintings and statues. "You really are a priest. I am surprised. I didn't know your… kind were the religious type. I thought it was just your cover."

"And what's your cover, doctor?" Issac responds, adding, "Anthropologist, astrophysicist, teacher, or is it, Watcher?"

Dr. Drago smiles. "You left so abruptly, I didn't have the chance to say the proper goodbye. So, what did you find up on the... what do you call it... the West Ridge?"

"Aren't you going to speak to me telepathically?" Issac asks.

"No need. No one is around. Besides, it takes too much energy. Concerned, too, you'll see my real thoughts. You really don't want to know what I am truly... thinking." Dr. Drago approaches a painting of Jesus. He stands before Him.

"You still didn't answer me," Issac says, moving toward him.

"About why I am here?" Dr. Drago says, turning toward Issac. "It is very coincidental that both of us are here, at this time, on this ranch." Dr. Drago turns back toward the painting. "Or is it... God remaining anonymous?"

"I thought you didn't believe in God."

Dr. Drago turns back toward Issac and faces him. "Ah, but I never said that. You read my thoughts. I am just searching for that nexus, the bridge to that true connection to..."

"God?" Issac asks. "Or Between Faith and Science, Matter and Dark Energy."

"Humans search for Dark Matter. You know what both of us are a part of, no matter how much you pray," Dr. Drago responds, examining other religious paintings.

"Well, I discovered Faith. How do you know we aren't a part of Him, too?" Issac replies.

Dr. Drago laughs. "Humans believe they are chosen and that doesn't include us. You know about the Book of Enoch."

"The Book that didn't make its way into the Bible?" Issac asks.

"Yes,' Dr. Drago says, gently touching a statue of an Archangel. "Enoch mentions us.

Remember? The Nephilim of the sky..."

"So, how do you believe we are a part of Creation?" Issac asks, adding, "I got that Archangel Michael statue from the shores of Galilee. It's carved from similar wood of that of Cross." Dr. Drago gently lifts his hand from the statue in a sign of respect.

"You know something. Don't you?" Issac says, about our connection with... Issac turns toward the painting of Jesus.

"I have a theory," Dr. Drago responds, gazing back toward the painting of Jesus, too, adding, "Do you really believe in the existence of God, Issac? Or is it just more of a hope."

"Yes, I believe," Issac says moving closer to the painting.

"I think you're still in the hoping stage. You see, if you believe, if you truly believe, there the power lies within…" Dr. Drago says, gazing into the eyes of Jesus. "I have a theory, it's just

mine, that God's been here all the time, regardless of the vessel; the humanoid body, the spirit, the type of dimensional warp of flexing time, even within the Quantium realm of space–time."

Dr. Drago approaches the lit candle before the altar. "Do you mind?" Issac looks at the flickering candle and Dr. Drago placing his hand through an arising flame, transforming it into a reptilian hand… Dr. Drago ShapeShifts–Issac sees in a full lengthen mirror, Dr. Drago becoming a Draconian Alien, yellow reptilian eyes, scaly purple tint skin.

"So, within that entity, Issac," Dr. Drago continues, "God emerges from our own creations, even universes from other aliens. We emerge while He's always been there, through a connection, through the Blood of Christ. That, my dear cousin, is what we all search for. That's why at all three levels there's that one connection, nexus, not between levels, but between the multiple creations of… God. It's interesting that He suffered so for humans, and yet, many do not appreciate what He did for them, while we search for that of which they were given."

"Do you think he is our savior?" Issac asks, his appearance ShapeShifting in the mirror next to Dr. Drago to that of an Alien Grey, Zeta Reticulum.

"That's why I am here, Issac. That's why I am here," Dr. Drago ends, ShapeShifting back to a human form along with Issac. "I am on a quest, the biggest one of all, to find our connection to," "Jesus," Issac adds as Dr. Drago goes up to the painting of Jesus. "We are all a part of Him."

"I've began investigating possible pathways at a quantum level for God to reveal Himself, during this era of time as He did in the past," Dr. Drago adds.

"God is revealing Himself," Issac says, adding, "You just have to look."

"Touché again, my cousin. Touché.. I didn't realize that Ancient Aliens was that complex of a show," Dr. Drago turns.

"You'd be surprised what's on T.V. these days," Issac says with a smile, "Do you truly believe, Jesus, once a man, is at the center of our universe? Multiple Universes?"

"Not just a man, Issac," Dr. Drago responds, adding, "Much bigger than that–He is God, the I AM. You know that, given your priestly duties. You see, we discovered that when we came to a realization of our own existence, not by any of our own webbed creations, but through Him. It's so simple, yet, so complex."

"Ah, it appears we're here for the same thing. In my research, what I have found, so far, correlates with what you theorize," Issac says with nod.

"I never said, it's just a theory, Issac. It seems like we're at different levels of our… research. You yearn to be what I am becoming closer to. You see, while you are conducting a study at your level, I am conducting a much more intrinsic one, with much more experience, and archeological dig of sorts, for Dark matter and what's within…"

"Within what, who?" Issac asks, as Dr. Drago begins to leave.

"Oh, I almost forgot. This is for you. Maybe you know him, a lost relative? Alas, poor Yorick…" Dr. Drago to tosses him the black backpack. Issac catches it. The door closes. Issac opens it–looks into the backpack–pulls out a bottle of cologne, razors. Appears confused…

In the desert of Arizona, driving across the sand, Christian rides in the back seat of the car with the mysterious driver, driving. Christian pulls out his phone and calls his commander.

"Yes, Lieutenant?" Christian's commander responds, over the phone, answering. "Sir. I just wanted to let you know, I am heading back to base as ordered. I should be there in a couple of hours, Christian says, holding his phone to his ear in the backseat.

"Who's orders? For what? I thought you were visiting your family?" The commander says, over the phone.

"Sir, I received a call to return to base from…" "From… who?"

"I am not sure," Christian says, lowering his phone, looking over at the black backpack. "Let me check… No. Nothing in the system about your return. What does your paperwork say about standby?"

"Hold on," Christian opens the black backpack. He appears shocked. "What the…" "Lieutenant?" The Commander says, Christian becoming silent. Christian pulls out the Peruvian Elongated Skull (a.k.a. Yorick). The driver turns around–His eyes ShapeShift to a reptilian yellow.

"Sorry, sir. You're not going back to base…" The driver says to him. UFO'S/AUP'S hover in the sky with unusual bright lights in the desert before them.

Flash of Light. The car vanishes being lifted into a beam of light in the sky. Empty silent desert. Darkness as the UFO'S/AUP'S fly off. Only the bright light of a full moon.

The Peruvian Elongated head falls from the sky, landing, rolling next to a cow's hollowed out carcass drained of blood… Vulture's circling– One cries out.

CHAPTER 7
Alien Hybrids, Greys, and Reptilians

Brandon, wearing sunglasses, pulls up in his jeep wrangler to the front of Red Rock High School with its top and sides open. Tommy approaches the jeep with a handful of books, folders.

"So this is your disguise? Sunglasses? You know you're not supposed to be up here, right." Tommy says, handing Brandon his school work.

"Why couldn't you have them just e-mail you this stuff?" Tommy asks.

Brandi appears walking across the campus, closely followed by Rocco. Tommy notices Brandon staring at Brandi.

"Oh, that's why," Tommy says. "You realize you're on long-term suspension. There's nothing higher than that."

"Yes. There's nothing higher than that," Brandon echoes, watching Brandi. "I am cool. I just wanted to see her."

"Yeah. I get it. But, you're not cool. Lately, dram seems to be following you for some reason," Tommy replies, adding. "Okay. You saw her. Now, you better get out of here before someone sees you. They thought I was bringing all this stuff to your house."

Shouting. Brandon and Tommy look over toward Brandi. She's face to face, arguing with Rocco. "Looks like there's trouble in paradise with your girl," Tommy says.

"She called me, last night," Brandon says, continuing to watch the argument, adding, But, I couldn't answer. I was preoccupied. So, did you find out anything?"

"About that teacher, Drago? No, bro. No one's even heard of him. Are you sure he's a teacher here?" Tommy says, watching the argument escalate as Brandi pushes Rocco in the chest. She throws up her hands, again, and walks away. Brandon pops the gear of his jeep in place, revs the engine. "Thanks for the work, bro."

"Hey, can you give me a lift?" Tommy asks.

]   "Sorry. I am only aloud to drive myself. I am not even aloud to take it to school. I have an agreement with my mom," Brandon says.

"Really? And here you are," Tommy says.

"Yes. Here I am," Brandon says. Tommy watches him drive away.

Brandon pulls his jeep up to Brandi walking alongside the road with a backpack over her shoulder. She sees Brandon pulling up next to her. She tries to ignore him, continuing to walk, acting like she doesn't notice him.

"Hey… Do you want a ride?" Brandon asks her. Brandi turns around, looks toward the school. She turns back. "Don't worry. You're far enough away, now. They can't see us."

"Am I allowed to be talking to you?" Brandi asks. "Aren't you on the no contact list or something. I thought was part of long-term suspensions."

"Why does everyone keep saying that? I can talk to whoever I want," Brandon says, gesturing for her to get in. Brandi goes to the front of the jeep, takes a picture of his license plate.

"What are you doing?" Brandon asks.

"Documenting. Just in case…" Brandi replies, tossing her backpack into the backseat.

"Just in case of what?" Brandon asks as she gets in. She fastens her seatbelt, smiles at Brandon and brushes back her long blonde hair.

"What were you saying?" Brandi asks, glancing at herself in the side mirror, putting lipstick on.

"I forget," Brandon says, pushing down on the accelerator, moving forward, Brandi's long beautiful blowing back in the wind.

"I didn't know you had a jeep," Brandi says.

"It's actually my brother's. He's in the airfare but let's me drive it once in a while." "Did you ever go on a date in it?" Brand asks with a smile, parting her hair away from her eyes, the distant mountains seemingly coming alive with a horizon of the sun.

"This is my first time," Brandon says, trying to keep his eyes on the empty open road. "First time for what?" Brandi asks, teasing him. "Are you telling me you never…"

"I am just saying…" Brandon says, pausing, "I don't know what I am saying."

"It seems like you're experiencing a lot of first times, recently. So, how do you like your suspension. I mean, you're getting time off, right?" Brandi says.

"I guess that's one way you can look at it," Brandon replies.

"I am sorry about what happened with Rocco and all," Brandi says looking toward the mountains. "We fight a lot."

"Then why do you stay with him?"

"Don't know, really. It's kind of complicated. One minute we're arguing and the next…" "But, it shouldn't have happened like that, just because you asked me to the prom."

"It wasn't your fault, not really his either. I shouldn't have asked you. I knew you had a boyfriend. I should have respected that," Brandon says, turning away from her.

"Then you would have never known," Brandi says a smile and a toss of her hair. "So, you'll go to the prom with me?" Brandon asks with a renewed enthusiasm. "We'll see," she says with a laugh. "So, how long are you suspended for?" "Indefinitely," Brandon simply responds, adding, "Kind of like my love life, not definite." Brandon responds back with a smile.

"Well, nothing's indefinite," Brandon says, touching his shoulder, adding, "Even the universe is finite."

"So, you know about the universe?" Brandon asks.

"Only part of it," Brandi replies, adding, "I like to explore, though." "So you are going to prom with me," Brandon says again.

"Your universe seems… interesting. I haven't met anyone like you," Brandi says, adding, "There are part of universes beyond my galaxy at Red Rock that I'd like to… experience." She gives him a glance, a look.

"Hey, turn here!" Brandi calls out at a fork in the road, pointing right. Brandon makes a sharp right turn, down a gravel less traveled dirt road.

"Don't we want to take the main paved road?" Brandon asks, bumping along the road, up and down, in the jeep. "Then we wouldn't be exploring our other universe," Brandi says as she stands and lifts up her arms in the wind.

"Hey, you better sit back down," Brandon says, trying to control the jeep.

"Or what? I'll get suspended?" Brandi laughs out, sitting back down, touching his hair.

"So, where does this road lead?" Brandon asks, excited by her touch.

"To another part of the universe… You act like you're afraid of me," Brandi says, caressing his hair and the side of his cheek.

"Do I have a reason to be afraid of you? So, really, where're you taking me?" Brandon asks, keeping his hands on the wheel, driving into thick, dense woods, upon a mountain.

"You're the one driving," Brandi says, pulling her hand away.

"Am I?" Brandon says, adding, "I didn't even known about this place." "You should explore more," Brandi says, adding, "So, have you ever…"

"Been on a date in this jeep? You're my first," Brandon says, going deeper into the woods, reaching over and taking hold of her hand.

"So is that a yes, for the prom?" Brandon asks again.

"Let's see where this road leads," Brandi responds, letting go of his hand as they come into a clearing, high atop a hill, overlooking a crystal clear blue pond with a cascading waterfall. Brandon stops the jeep. "Wow. This is amazing…" Brandon says as Brandi grabs her backpack, jumps out of the jeep, and runs toward the pond. Brandon watches as she drops the backpack at the edge of the water, takes off all her clothes, and carefully walks into the pond. Naked, she dives in–"Don't worry, Tommy. I am going in," Brandon says to himself–Jumps out of his jeep.

Brandon goes up to the edge of the pond–watching Brandi swim naked through the crystal clear water, doing twists and turns, stretching her bare legs out above the surface, as she disappears beneath the reflections of the trees' branches above her, fading in and out within a glistening sunlight. She pops her head above the surface–"What are you waiting for! Come in!"

Brandon hesitantly takes off his clothes as Brandi swims freestyle arm over arm across the clear pond–toward the waterfall. He watches her get out, climb up upon the rocks, and, gingerly tippy-toe behind the cascading waterfall, exposing emerging scars, marks, upon her in the light through the flowing water, a beauty of reptilian-like, *Tiger Stripes.*

Mesmerized–Brandon enters the water and moves toward her, diving in and swimming across the pond–He remembers his mother's words, far deep beneath the surface–" You are different, my son… God is in you…" Brandon emerges up from the pond, breaking through the water's surface on the other side. He gets out and climbs up onto the rocks behind the waterfall. He looks for her. But, she's not there. Then, suddenly, Brandi appears behind him. She laughs, resting both her arms on his shoulders.

"How did you do that?" Brandon asks with a returned laugh. "Do what?" Brandi says, continuing to tease him.

"Appear out of nowhere like that, and look like..." he says turning around and facing her. She gazes into his eyes. He briefly notices her beautiful green eyes appear *not human, reptilian.* Brandon leans in to kiss her. They kiss, then–She pushes him away.

"Not yet, bad boy on suspension," she says, her eyes turning back to that of a human, yet, still green, the reptilian stripes, scares images fading away with the cascading waterfall. Brandon is amazed, staring at her beautiful toned, wet, body, wanting to kiss and caress every inch of her.

"Do you like what you see?" Brandi asks, placing a soft touch up against his chest. "Come on," Brandi says to him telepathically. "Did you just tell me to, come on?"

Brandon responds verbally, surprised at her interfacing thoughts. "Yes," she responds in thought.

Brandon lets out a large smile and follows her, further up the rocks behind the waterfall. When they get to the top, atop the hill above the waterfall, she lies down on her back and stares up toward the sky. Brandon lies down next to her... looking up.

"The answers are all up there," Brandi says to him, pointing toward the sky. "The answers to what?" Brandon asks, wondering.

"Why we're here... The patterns all around the universe show efficiency of an energy flow. So, when nature, energy finds an efficient way to do something, it repeats the process."

"Like with you," Brandon says, turning and gazing at her, adding, "You're so beautiful." "You have to look at the sky," she replies.

"I am," he responds to her, looking into her eyes. "I am looking at something the universe found a way to be... so, so beautiful..."

They kiss... Brandi points, again, up toward the sky.

"You see, Brandon. The universe is connected, everywhere. Earth itself is similar across all scales no matter the size or object because you will always see the same exact patterns. The universe's smaller processes are mirror images of the larger ones and vise versa. In the Egyptian times, it was called, the law of correspondence, meaning what is above is a mirror image of what is below. Brandi turns back toward Brandon, reaching out, she touches his chest.

"You can understand the universe by understanding the human body," she says to him. "I'd love to understand the universe," he responds to her gentle touch.

"I'm sure you do. I've picked up on your... electro-magnetic vibration," Brandi says with a smile and a slight downward cast of her eyes. Brandi begins moving her fingers around his firm sculptured chest in geometrical, symbolic patterns as an encircling hurricane just forming far off in the distant parts of a hidden sea amidst the backdrop of the sounds of the cascading waterfall.

"You see, Brandon. The world has a firmament, the electric magnetic field around your heart is the same as the one around the earth and galaxies. It can go as small as a magnet to something as large as a super cluster of two-hundred thousand galaxies; one heart entrainment within the three hearts of creation..."

Brandon gently clasps upon her hand. "One heart from three? How can that be? Aren't we created from two people with two hearts? I don't understand what all this all means..." He gently kisses her hand and lets go. "Unless you're talking about some kind of genetic infusion of DNA or something..."

Brandi points toward the sky. "The magnetic field around earth is shaped as a bull. This explains why brain cells look similar to the cosmic web, and why eyes look like the shape of nebulas. It occurs because the universe is a fractal, geometric pattern. Three becomes one..."

Brandon sits up and looks down at her. "Where did you learn all of this stuff?" Brandi sits up and faces him. She smiles. "My dad works for NASA."

"Did your dad ever mention the existence of aliens? I always wonder if they really exist. I mean, since he works at NASA, he must have heard stories, right?" Brandon asks. Brandi turns away as Brandon continues, "According to Tommy, there are primarily three kinds of aliens, the Grey's, Nordics, and... Reptilians. Brandi turns back.

"I didn't know Tommy was an expert in other forms of life. Didn't he get a D in science?

No. My father didn't mention anything like that," Brandi says, standing up, looking down at Brandon. In the sunlight, with her still somewhat wet body, glistening, he can see slight images.

"I think we should be respectful to all forms of life, their feelings, their own hopes and dreams, their… passions," Brandi says, reaching down to take Brandon's hand, helping him up.

"We're all part of God, not just aliens…" she says drawing him close, adding, "Well, my dad didn't say anything about the Zeta Reticulan or the Nordics… But, he did tell me about the fractal, geometrical patterns and said the Reptilians wouldn't be able to come here to earth because it's too dense. They wouldn't be able to… function." She places her hand again on his chest as Brandon appears confused.

"Really? So, they do exist?" Brandon asks with a smile, nod, and kiss on his chest from Brandi. "I always wondered why there are so many pictures of Reptilians in ancient cultures."

"They're not true Reptilians, just, well, their puppets. Since they can't enter earth's atmosphere, they communicate and manipulate people under their control to do their will."

"They can control us?" Brandon asks as Brandi begins encircling her finger again upon his chest, creating tingles up and down his spine.

"Yes. They can control humans, like puppets. When they do their eyes become yellow with inverted pupils as they connect to the transferable electromagnetically charged coil membranes of…" Brandi's eyes appear to invert, turn yellow… Brandon shakes his head.

"That's crazy. You're messing with me," Brandon says as Brandi simply replies, "Absolutely, I am messing with you…"

"About what? The existence of aliens?"

"About Reptilians, silly boy. Of course they can sometimes… enter earth's atmosphere," Brandi smiles with a slap on Brandon's bare buttocks. "Come on, I'll race you back. Try to keep up…" "To where? Reality?" Brandon asks, feeling left behind within the previous thoughts and points of their conversation.

Brandi smiles and jumps back into the pond, laughing loudly as she breaks through the surface. Brandon hesitates but follows… the waterfall flowing down into the crystal clear blue pond. Their heads emerge, through the surface of the water, closely facing each other.

"You see, we're the same," she says to him, nose to nose. She turns and swims toward the sandy white banks. Walking out of the pond, Brandi goes over to her clothes and picks them up as Brandon swims toward her, walking out of the pond, approaching her.

"Ugh. They're all wet," Brandi says, examining her clothes. "Can you give me my tee- shirt? It's right next to you, inside my backpack."

Brandon reaches down and opens the backpack. He briefly looks up, sees a reflection of Brandi in the pond–*Tiger Stripes… They slowly fade as he turns toward her.*

"What's the matter?" Brandi asks.

"Nothing," Brandon replies, searching again in the backpack. Shocked, he pulls out a Reptilian Hand wrapped in plastic.

"What's this?" Brandon asks, holding it up, "Some kind of Halloween prop?"

"Oh, that's just something my father gave me. He said, it would keep me safe, kind of like a warning… to something, don't know," Brandi says, appearing defensive.

"To who?" Brandon says, examining the hand.

Brandi shies away, saying, "Did you find my tee-shirt?"

Brandin carefully places the hand back and takes out a pink tee-shirt. He tosses it to her.

She puts it on, pulling it down over her head, barely covering her upper part of her thighs.

She looks up. Bright Purple Lights hovering above them. "I think we should go," she says, shielding her eyes with her hand as a cast of purple overtakes the pond. Brandon looks up. The sun is too bright. He looks away as Brandi takes him by his hand and leads him back toward the jeep. "Let's hurry," she adds.

Just as they get to the jeep, Brandi pauses and turns. "Oh, did you get my backpack?" Brandon turns back and goes to get her backpack by the side of the pond.

"Hurry, Brandon!"

Brandon gets to the side of the pond and picks up Brandi's backpack. Strong wind. He gazes up–Bright Purple Lights, moving closer toward him. "What the…" He runs back to the jeep, hands Brandi her backpack and jumps into the driver's side. "Come on." Brandi gets in. Brandon backs up the jeep, twists the steering wheel, shifts into drive, presses down on the accelerator and takes off with gravel stones flying off…

"They're coming," Brandi says, carefully placing her backpack into the backseat. "Who's coming?" Brandon asks.

"Never mind. Let's just keep going, faster…" Brandi says as Brandon presses down further on the accelerator…

A Reptilian Alien, about seven-feet tall, purple scaly skin, dark slanted eyes, long fingers and a elongated jaw, stands by the side of the pond. He looks toward the the pathway, the road.

Brandi looks toward Brandon. "So, are you afraid of me, now? Because of what you found." The jeep bounces, moving upon rocks and stones on less driven path.

"No," Brandon responds. "I was afraid of you before, remember? When I asked you to the prom," Brandon says with a smile, letting up on pushing down on the accelerator.

"So, what's your real story?" Brandi says, glancing back at her backpack. "Story?" Brandon asks.

"Yeah. About who you really are... You seem different. I noticed it when you swam toward me at the pond," Brandi says, turning back, looking ahead as they ride down the path, into a deeper, brighter, part of the woods with a wider road, less bumpy as the jeep calms from tossing and turning.

"I could ask you the same thing," Brandon says, adding, "I don't think that hand is a prop and, when I swam across the pond I saw..."

"Saw what?" Brandi asks.

Brandon pauses, glances over at Brandi and replies, "The most beautiful woman I've ever seen in my life..." Brandi smiles, leans over, and kisses him on the cheek.

"So, tell me... your story," Brandon says. "You go first," Brandi replies.

"How do I know if I tell you my story, then you'll actually tell me your's?" Brandon asks. "You don't. That's life, right? The unknown," Brandi responds.

"Well, my story," Brandon says with a pause and a breath, "To tell you the truth, I am not sure what my story is. My m other keeps inferring stuff. But, I never really know what she's talking about."

"You must know something... about who you are, besides... what I know now," Brandi says with a smile, touching his shoulder. I don't think you're afraid of anything. You definitely are different. Maybe your mother wants you to find out who you are by yourself."

"Maybe... Anything is possible, right? All I know is that I grew up on a ranch, went to school, got straight A's, met a hot girl. That's about it so far, oh, and I have a hotshot fighter pilot brother. My mom, my brother, they're my family. My father went missing. He taught me a lot though… I really miss him. He was teaching me to be a fighter pilot, too, before…"

"What happened to him?" Brandi asks.

"I don't like to talk about it. When I do, it opens up a lot within me," Brandon says, gazing blankly ahead as they break free of the tree line and into the open of a more traveled road.

"I understand," Brandi says, brushing back her long hair in the breeze, adding, "I don't even know who my father is. My mother tells me stories. But, sometimes, I think she is just making them up. Whenever I ask about my father, she becomes defensive and, in a way, fearful. Don't know why…"

"Did she ever say what happened to him?" Brandon asks.

"Every time I try to find out more about him, she just changes the subject… But, your story, about growing up on a ranch and learning to be a fighter pilot, sounds like a great story, to me. You have a good opportunity to…" Brandi says, flirting, adjusting the bottom hem of her short pink tee-shirt. Brandon notices, takes his eyes off the road…

"Watch out!" Brandi cries out.

Brandon slams on the breaks–looks up–A CYLINDRICAL UFO, CIGAR-SHAPED, HOVERING BEFORE THEM. Brandon appears shocked. Brandi leans over, places her hands upon Brandon's cheeks, turns his head toward her and kisses him. As she does, it creates a Blue Aura around them, as if a shield, protecting them. Brandon embraces Brandi. The UFO flies off.

The waterfall cascades down into the pond in a beautiful cast of blue, dissolving the purple tint, becoming brighter and clearer with images of Brandi's and Brandon's embrace being visible in the pond… The trees sway, sounds of a distant echo roll upon the winds… toward the sky, toward a destiny written long before…

CHAPTER 8
The East Ridge, East Side, Mirror of the West

Crystal and I drive up in my Monster pick-up truck alongside Issac and the other ranchers, sitting upon horses, overlooking the East Ridge of the ranch. Issac points toward large Circular Symbols embedded in the soil.

"Looks like it's happened here, too," Issac says to me through my truck window, adding, "See. Right down there."

"Where do you think they're really coming from?" I ask, seeing them far below as if gazing through a lens of a telescope back into my past.

"They're probably just from kids… All of this is probably just from kids," Crystal blurts out while staring at herself in the truck's side mirror—through a different lens of a past. She takes out bright red lipstick, begins putting it on, thick, along with mascara and eyeliner.

"Kids wouldn't know how to do that, make those kinds of symbols," Issac says, pulling back on the reigns of his horse, adding, "Let's take a closer look, shall we?" Issac glances over at Crystal with her full make-up on. He appears suddenly drawn to her, sensing a lure, a sexually driven magnetic connection. "Do you want to ride down with me, Ma'am?"

"I don't do horses," Crystal replies, acting disinterested, turning back toward the mirror. "Sorry, Ma'am," Issac says, kicking his horse with his spurs. Crystal turns away from glancing at herself and watches Issac ride off with the other ranchers following.

"He sure knows how to control a horse," Crystal says with a sense of admiration and renewed bewilderment.

"Do you have a thing for Issac, now?" I ask with a sarcastic smile, adding, "I think he's beginning to like you."

"Yes… Let's go take a closer look at what's going on, shall we," Crystal says with a returned smile, adding, "at the… symbols."

"I think my whore sister is returning," I laugh out.

"Maybe," Crystal says with a dab of her lipstick on her upper part of her side lip.

I shift my Monster truck into gear and drive down into the East Ridge Valley below. The canyon seems colored in a bluish grey, a tint of a haze, mirrored within a circular lens of a scope as if traveling back into a another time. Crystal with her make-up on, reminded me of that time in the past when I wanted to experience what it was like to open up and explore what was beating inside of me, that distant part of myself, the East Side where my fantasies lived only in a bluish grey tint of a haze until…

Issac gets down off his horse and touches the symbols in the dirt as the other ranchers remain upon their horses, encircling him. Crystal and I pull up behind them in my truck. We get out and approach Issac.

"They look exactly like the ones on the West Ridge," Issac says continuing to examine the symbols as I imagine my West and East Sides colliding.

"How can that be?" I ask, reflecting upon my past and my own residual of compartments encompassing my inner self, my emotions, my analytical, my logical, then, my uncontrollable fantasies, spurless, wild, bucking, running abandon across the desert–*like Blaze.*

"How can that be?" I ask, trying to put boundaries within all of my own compartments where East Side stays, well, on it's own side–away from *the West.*

"Well, it's simple. Whatever landed on the West Side, landed here, too," Issac replies, standing up, turning and staring at Crystal, adding. "They seem to be attracted, to your ranch."

"They?" Crystal asks, staring back at him. "Yes. Them," Issac responds to Crystal's look.

That Night…It, That, What, Oh my God, Them…

"That Night…It, That, What, Oh my God, Them…" I say to myself as Issac walks up to Crystal and faces her. "These symbols, they look different than those on the West Side, I mean Ridge," I say, noticing, adding, "They look like a fish."

"It will be alright," Issac says to Crystal, "I'll protect you." "From what?" I answer, gazing at all the symbols.

"You know, Maria," Crystal says to me, adding, "They've come back." "For who?" I ask, feeling shaken.

"Probably for you, Maria or… Brandon," Crystal says, coming over and standing by my side, adding, "You know this was going to happen sooner or later. Even Issac knows."

Issac sympathetically nods. He then gestures to the other ranchers. They turn their horses and ride away as Issac moves toward Maria and stands next to her, too.

"These symbols tell a story," Issac says, looking upward toward the sky. "I noticed too, the symbol of the fish. It's a story heading into a final act."

"Should we let the sheriff know?" I ask, as if I was the one, again, as permission, tied to that metallic table in a submissive position.

Issac dominantly answers, taking the reigns of his horse, "She'll just come out, again, take a few pictures, do a report. Just a waste of time, if you ask me." He gets up on his horse.

"I'd like to let her know, anyway. Give her a heads up just in case," I say, trying to take back some kind of control and finally break free from being bound to the trauma of my past.

"Over here!" One of the ranchers cries out in the distance, dismounted from his horse, standing over something. The other ranchers dismount and encircle him. Issac turns his horse and gallops toward them as Crystal and I jump into my truck, start it up, and ride after them.

I ride up to all the ranchers, including Issac, standing around a dead cattle's carcass. We get out and go up to them. Crystal approaches and takes hold of Issac's arm, stunned, covering her mouth. I look down at it, it's hollow mutilate carcass—no signs of blood or organs. Crystal lets go of Issac's arm and approaches it in a shallow ravine. She stoops down and examines it.

"It looks like this poor animal has been completely gutted," Crystal says, "I've never seen anything like this before, even in med school."

"What do you think did it?" I ask, adding, "Some kind of predator?"

"A predator wouldn't be able to do this. There's no blood, no remnants of organs. The brain… looks like it was sucked out of the skull through this small opening."

"So whatever did this, eats brains?" I ask.

"It appears that way," Crystal says as Issac returns to gazing up into the sky. "Why do you keep looking up to the sky, Issac?" I ask.

"I am praying," Issac replies to me, adding, "We have to get ready."

"For what?" I ask, sensing the merging of my *West and East Side of my past.*

Another rancher, a hundred feet away, suddenly, calls out to us. We simultaneously turn and run over toward him. He stands at the base of a gully next to a small creek. Looking down, we see hollowed out remains of numerous mutilated cattle, motionless in a shallow rippling moving stream...

Looking down, gazing through a time tunnel spinning into my past, I realize that the West and East Sides within me are actually one in a linear, yet, abstract connection. I am both of them, a dichotomy of a motionless, yet, a moving phenomenon of time, ticking, existing, beating... The fantasies of me being that persona are interwoven amidst the same dynamic of being a learned astrophysicist. The explorations were not separate, rather they were in a symbiotic, symphonic melody orchestrating together, rippling through space, sending signals to entities trillions of light years away... and now, as the solar eclipse within myself is complete, I am one. I am the young woman in the cheerleading outfit and the mother of a gifted son and fighter pilot. Who I am, is not as important, now, as what I am. I must find a way, to connect through prayer, like Issac, with the spirit of our Lord redeems us to do so. For I am what He made me, made us in the images of a soul. I am... I remember my father's words from long ago, as I gaze toward that shallow rippling moving stream...

"Maria," Crystal says awakening me, "Are you okay?"

"Yes, yes. I am fine. Thanks," I respond, imaging myself still curled up in my bed, back in Manhattan, clasping upon those Red Rosary Beads... the clock ticking–1:11 am...

Time. What is it? Some physicists believe it is a mere an illusion, a fragment of what we, ourselves, perceive that to be real within our own subjectivity hidden within our minds. Yet, according to my own research and observations, prior to my indulged explorations within, I found that time is much different from that of which we perceive to be true or, rather, real. It is more like a dimension, outside the realm of our own three dimensional reality involving three planes, the X, the Y, and the Z. Time is essentially in a fourth dimension, like Einstein said. It is intertwined like my *East and West Sides* within a *Space/Time continuum.* This all directly correlates to relativity in which time and space are connected. Dilation in time is a principle that states time slows the faster the velocity. So, if we could travel deep in space for a year or so, when we came back to earth, decades would have passed, here. They did movies about this, along with time travel, warping of spacetime, traveling through wormholes… To me, though, it's even much more complex. Some have theorized that time is on-going simultaneously, existing in orbs. It is not linear, but rather, abstract. The 1800's is occurring at the same time next to us in this era in an encircling orb. I felt this when I was aboard their ship, the warping and bending of time. They found a way to do this, to move things through ceilings and walls, by way of, bending time…

As I turn away from the rippling of the stream and the cast images of drained cattle, I search for an inner peace of hope, one in which I can find the answers to what really happened to me a couple of decades ago. I can still feel their touch, imagine their cold dark stares, their unmoving non-existent emotions, locked into forcing me to go where I yearned not to move.

Time. What is that of which we do not know? And yet, it controls us, it absorbs us into an unknown reality where they exist, far beyond that of those remnants of knowledge who came before us. What are the answers, I do not know. But, I know my son will soon… My hope lies with him. He is different. God is within him…

CHAPTER 9
Space, Velocity, and Time

A Grandfather's Clock chimes in the dining room of the ranch house as Brandon enters through the front door. He glances in and sees Dr. Drago, sitting quietly at the dining room table, reading a book. He holds it up as Brandon approaches him.

"What are you doing here?" Brandon asks, holding folders.

"Reading, 'The Realm of Quantum Physics,'" Dr. Drago answers, holding up the book, adding, "I am your tutor, remember?"

"I didn't know we had a session, today," Brandon says confused, adding, "My mother didn't say anything."

"No time like the present, that is, going by human's time," Dr. Drago adds with a smile.

Dr. Drago glances up at the clock–The Chimes top. "Man made time. Interesting, isn't it? I guess your mother didn't get my message about beginning today. Is that your work from school?" Brandon clutches the folders in his hands, his school work Tommy gave him.

"Yes," Brandon answers.

"Well, you won't be needing them," Dr. Drago says, rising. "Don't I have to turn these in?" Brandon asks.

"You don't have to do anything. You ultimately create your own electromagnetic fields, your own reality for your life, Brandon. It's all within you."

"What's within me?" Brandon asks, placing the folders down upon the table. "Everything," Dr. Drago replies, "Everything... So, are you ready for your lesson about electromagnetic fields and folds in time?" Brandon hesitantly nods. "Great. Let's go," Dr. Drago says, beginning to exit. "Where to?" Brandon asks.

"On a class field trip," Dr. Drago responds with a smile, walking out of the ranch house with Brandon following closely behind.

"Do you have a vehicle of transportation?" Dr. Drago asks, pausing in front of the house. "Yeah, my jeep," Brandon points over to his jeep. "I just filled it up with gas."

"Looks like you took it for an… off road field trip of your own," Dr. Drago says, moving toward it. He gets into the passenger side and notices a tube of lipstick on the floor. Brandon gets into the driver's side.

"Yeah, I just took it for a spin, up in the mountains. I went Bird watching," Brandon says as Dr. Drago picks up the tube of lipstick. He hands it to Brandon.

"I am sure you enjoyed… watching her," Dr. Drago says with a wider smile. He glances into the backseat, notices Brandi's backpack. "Is that your's?"

"Oh, that's my friend's. She must have left it," Brandon says.

"Do you know what's in there? I sense something," Dr. Drago says. "Like what?" Brandon asks, adding, "Probably just perfume and stuff."

"Something more, something different," Dr. Drago stares at it as Brandon imagines the reptilian hand. "Do you think she would mind if we took a look? Maybe something crawled into it. I smell something dead," Dr. Drago says, trying to convince Brandon to look inside.

"We can't just look into someone else's backpack," Brandon says. "Why not?" Dr. Drago asks.

"Because, isn't that unethical? Aren't you supposed to be a teacher?" Brandon asks.

"Ah, but I am also your mentor," Dr. Drago answers, adding, "There's a difference. What if, what if there's something in there that can change your life? Would you look, then?"

"How…" Brandon appears confused.

"If you open it, look into it, and close it, how will she ever know?" "I'll know," Brandon replies.

"And if you… know. How does that matter in the grand course of history?" Dr. Drago responds, adding, "So, if your destiny is in that bag, you won't open it because you will know you did? That's not logical."

"But, it's ethical. My mom taught me ethics," Brandon counters. "Who's ethics?" Dr. Drago asks.

"What's right and wrong ethics," Brandon replies. "Who's right and wrong?" Dr. Drago counters back.

"I am not opening Brandi's backpack," Brandon affirms.

"Alas, Brandi. Now, I know her name, your star. That's better than knowing what's in her backpack. We can go, now. Do you know how to drive this thing?" Dr. Drago asks.

"You did all that just to find out her name?" Brandon asks.

"Yes," Dr. Drago responds, adding, "And to see if you have ethics. You were willing to give up even your destiny for the girl you love. Maybe I can help you capture your star."

"What's that supposed to mean… and how do you know I love her?"

"Because of, well, you'll find out. I'll honor, though, your respect for her… backpack," Dr. Drago says with a smile, adding, "Besides. I already know what's in it."

"How?" Brandon asks.

"Because of what you'll find out," Dr. Drago simply says, "Because of that… Let's go.

That way, Brandon," Dr. Drago points toward the West Ridge. They drive onward…

"So, do you have a driver's license, to drive this primitive thing?" Dr. Drago asks. "A learner's permit," Brandon says with a smile.

"Good enough," Dr. Drago responds as they drive across the desert of the ranch's spanning acreage. Brandon gazes out toward the mountain ridge, the purple cast in the light of a bluish hue. The sun is partially hidden behind unusual clouds as Brandon, momentarily, sees an image of something darting in and out between them. Dr. Drago notices.

"So, tell me, Brandon. How did you really learn about Vesica Piscis? I know you like gym class, too," Dr. Drago says with a smile.

"I read about it… after my dad left." "Where did he go?"

"No one knows. We don't know if he left or…" Brandon begins to say, looking away from the clouds and toward Dr. Drago. "That's when I really wanted to understand how everything works. I know it sounds crazy, but I thought if I can figure out how the universe interacts with everything then somehow…"

"You would find your father…" Dr. Drago finishes as Brandon nods with a tear.

"Well, I don't know if you know this, but the Vesica Piscis is Latin, meaning Vessel of the Fish. It's symbolized by two circles of equal diameters, overlaying them in a way that their circumferences cross each other's epicenters. It is the most visible symbol in your human culture, spanning religions and various architecture throughout history," Dr. Drago says, staring ahead.

"My human culture?" Brandon asks, adding, "Isn't it your's too?"

"My culture is difficult to understand here… in Arizona. I come from a much more complex realm," Dr. Drago says.

"New York?" Brandon asks.

"Well, let's just say, it's outside Manhattan," Dr. Drago says with a wider smile. "Let's just keep going…"

As they continue to drive across the open desert, the object following them darts away.

Brandon catches a glimpse of it cutting in a ninety-degree angle.

"Wow, did you see that?" Brandon asks, adding, "I wonder what that is… I saw something like that when…" Dr. Drago glances back at the backpack.

"When you were with Brandi?" Dr. Drago responds. Brandon looks at him, pauses. "Yes, when I was with Brandi," Brandon says, gripping tighter on the steering wheel. "Don't worry about them, Brandon," Dr. Drago says, looking up. "You're much more powerful than… them."

"Who are they?" Brandon asks.

"You can say, my neighbors… just outside Manhattan," Dr. Drago laughs.

The sun blends with intermittent clouds as the mountains grow to a hovering length as the wind blows, moving debris of vegetation with a mirage of other worlds crossing before them. As they stand atop the West Ridge, looking down into the canyon, the both see the Geometrically Aligned Fish-Symbols, the same symbols Issac and others examined.

"What do those symbols mean? Where did they actually come from? Brandon asks.

"If I tell you where they came from, then you'll know what I mean. The one thing you'll learn about me, Brandon is that I'd rather have my students discover for themselves the true answers. It's kind of like taking a test. If I just give you the answers then you won't learn anything. You must find out for yourself the… true answers.

"Are there false answers?" Brandon asks, appearing confused.

"To some," Dr. Drago answers, gazing down into the canyon. Dr. Drago, suddenly, turns. He notices a Blue Lit Dome nestled atop the ridge a few hundred yards away. He gestures toward it. "What's over there?"

Brandon turns toward the Dome upon an elevated hill, overlooking the canyon below. "It's nothing," Brandon answers, adding, It's just a clubhouse our dad built for us as kids."

"It looks like a remarkable… clubhouse. Mind if I take a look?" Dr. Drago asks. Brandon hesitates but nods. They get back into the jeep and drive up the small hill.

Parking in front of it, the Dome is unusual, a bluish hue shade of color and metallic tint. They get out of the jeep and approach the Blue Dome. Dr. Drago goes up to it, places his hand upon it. In a brief moment, with an unusual cast of light, Dr. Drago's hand appears reptilian, like Brandi's in the backpack. He pulls it away, appears human again…

"Are you aware your clubhouse can fly, Brandon?"

"It's just a metal dome over some dirt. Nothing else, really," Brandon says, defensively.

"Something's hidden there that can change your life," Dr. Drago says, glancing back at the jeep, adding, "You should have opened your friend's backpack, Brandon. It all begins by opening that galactic, magnetic doorway to your destiny…"

"In Brandi's backpack?" Brandon asks as Dr. Drago opens a large unusual metallic door and enters with Brandon closely following.

Brandon reaches over, knowing where it is, and flicks a switch. Lights come on with a soft humming sound of a control panel.

"It's a very technologically filled clubhouse, Brandon."

"Just lights and whistles our dad put together for us, to play with. They don't do much," Brandon answers, cautiously walking further in.

"When was the last time you were in here?" Dr. Drago asks, gazing around at all the panels and technological machinery.

"It's been a while, since my dad went missing," Brandon says, glancing over at a large spanning control panel with two metallic shaped chairs before it. Dr. Drago goes over and sits down in one of the chairs before the instruments.

"Did you father ever tell you what these instruments can do?" Dr. Drago asks, placing his hands upon them, reflecting images of the reptilian hand. "You know they really aren't toys."

"Yes. I know. We figured it out," Brandon finally admitted. "When we were kids." Brandon flashes back to when he and Christian were young, sitting before the instrument panel. Christian begins pressing the buttons. The dome begins to shake, move…

Brandon cries out, "Stop Christian!"

"I'm trying! But, I don't know how!" Christian responds back, frantically pressing more buttons. An adult hand, suddenly, reaches out from behind them and presses one button. The dome calms. They turn around. Their father stands behind them, smiling…

Dr. Drago sits before the instruments within the dome, staring at Brandon. Dr. Drago is smiling. "I see. Your dad saved you. You must have been scared. What would have both of you done if this… clubhouse took of?"

"You can read my mind?" Brandon asks, shocked.

"Yes… and so can you, once you learn. You're gifted," Dr. Drago says, turning away from the panel as Brandon begins to leave.

"Wait," Dr. Drago calls out, adding, "Don't worry. I don't invade your other thoughts.

They are safe, the ones for Brandi…"

Brandon turns back. "How can you focus on just some thoughts?"

"It's like talking. You send out signals, but only the ones your thinking at that moment in time," Dr. Drago explains, adding, "I can't just explore everything your thinking… only that of which you wish to communicate. It just skips the articulated verbal phase…"1

"Okay," Dr. Drago replies. "Okay, what?" Brandon asks.

"I'll stay out of all your thoughts," Dr. Drago replies, adding, "You just said to." "I did?" Brandon asks.

"You thought it," Dr. Drago ends. "Let's get back to work and begin the lesson." "You're searching for Dark Matter, here on earth," Brandon blurts out with Dr. Drago's hands upon the instruments.

"Very good, Brandon… You just read my mind. Now, don't go too far down that rabbit hole of my thoughts. You may be shocked at what you may discover. Come." Dr. Drago gestures to the seat next to him. Brandon sits down next to Dr. Drago.

"Do you know how this clubhouse flies?" Dr. Drago asks. Brandon shakes his head, staring at all the instruments.

"We stop pushing the buttons after what happened," Brandon replies.

"You should never stop exploring, Brandon. That's what keeps you moving, through life.

This ship uses Element-115, from Supernovas. It provides a fold in the time, space continuum which acts as kind of a wave guide for Electromagnetic Energy…"

"To counteract gravity," Brandon adds.

"Yes. Very good, Brandon. You just have done your homework."

"So, are you going to teach me how to fly this…" Brandon begins to ask.

"No," Dr. Drago replies, adding, "You're going to have to learn to fly it yourself, like life.

I am just going to give your the knowledge of the tools in order for you to explore and learn. Besides, you don't have that kind of learner's permit to fly this ship," Dr. Drago says, smiling.

Dr. Drago examines more closely the control panel. "I just need to use its communication system, for now." Dr. Drago examines the instruments on the panel.

"Why are you really here?" Brandon asks.

Dr. Drago pauses, then continues examining the panel. He moves switches and turns instruments, lights flash on the console an assortment of various colors with each move, each turn, each twist. "I've been sent to coordinate a secret program, for the government… my day job, if you will, besides being a tutor."

"Then why don't you just do that, the government job?" Brandon asks.

"Because being a teacher, your mentor, keeps me actually more closely connected to the universe. Sometimes the smallest things can have the biggest impacts," Dr. Drago responds focusing in on another smaller instrument with a touch.

"Oh, like the Butterfly Effect," Brandon says.

"What'a a butterfly?" Dr. Drago asks. Brandon takes a step back.

"It's an insect that changes into a butterfly," Brandon replies, cautiously. Dr. Drago appears to have a blank look on is face, his eyes begin to shift.

"Yes. Butterflies. From the lepidopteran superfamily Papilionoidea. They have bright colored wings…" The bright colors of the panel become more prominent.

"Did you just look that up, in your mind?" Brandon asks, adding "Are you one of them?" "Depends," Dr. Drago responds.

"Depends on what?" Brandon asks.

"What them you are talking about," Dr. Drago says with a slight turn of his head. "The program that your working on, is it related to me somehow?" Brandon asks. "Let's just say that I'm on a type of suspension, too, and was given work to complete, assignments in a way, just like you," Dr. Drago responds. "Like what?" Brandon asks.

"Ah, yes. That's part of your lesson, your exploration. You know Brandon, when I met you, I didn't expect you to be, well, so gifted. It's like observing a far off planet. You meticulously gather information, make precise calculations, examine the atmosphere and environment, and yet, when you get closer, you see something much more different than what you were studying from afar."

"So, you are here for me."

"You don't realize it. But, you have God in you, genesis-driven elements of Creation, various constructs of Dark Matter… It's kind of complicated. But, in time, you'll learn."

"My mom told me I have God in me. But, doesn't everyone? If they choose to accept Him?" Brandon asks.

"Some are more powerful than others. It's a choice but also a predestine," Dr. Drago says, adding, "However, that's my own personal theory. Others may have different perspective on the matter. Others meaning, human others not them others," Dr. Drago adds with a smile and glance.

Dr. Drago more intensely manipulates the instruments. The lights–of the instruments, now, flicker in a type of Alien Morse Code like the lights back at NYU two decades ago.

"Okay, I'll explain it in more simpler terms. Let's say, you're the Center, Brandon, of a Metatron Cube. Years ago, let's say we infused your mother with streams of energy, DNA from three types of alien species, the Grey's, Nordics, and…"

"Reptilians?" Brandon asks.

"Yes. We prefer other names such as Draconians," Dr. Drago says.

"Three hearts are one, Grey's, Nordics, and Draconians," Brandon theorizes.

"You got it. You're a good student, Brandon. I am going to really enjoy mentoring you," Dr. Drago says, reaching out his hand toward the instruments. His hand transforms clearly into a reptilian hand. Brandon, stunned and shaken, gets up, pushing away his chair.

"Why are you acting like this. You figured it out moments ago," Dr. Drago says calmly. "Tommy was right. I knew you weren't a real teacher. You're a… reptilian."

"I told you, a Draconian. There's a difference… and why can't you have a tutor, a teacher from… outside Manhattan. I am teaching you, correct?" Dr. Drago says, turning, standing. "Does a teacher just have to be human? There are many types of teachers, Brandon. We can all learn from other entities. Dogs teach us how to protect and love unconditionally. Lions teach us how to lead. Wolves teach us how to survive in a pack… Look at the world around you, Brandon… and now look at the universe, beyond Manhattan. We too learn, love, seek."

"What are you seeking?" Brandon asks.

"The Truth," Dr. Drago responds, saying again, "The Truth, Brandon." "And what is Truth," Brandon asks.

"I may not know what a butterfly is. But, I do know what you just asked me can be found in special book," Dr. Drago replies.

"What book?" Brandon asks.

"The Bible, Brandon. Seek the Truth and it shall set you free," Dr. Drago said, adding, "Many will be coming here, soon, Brandon. They're all seeking, searching for the Higher entity, a re-connection to the Source of Creation, the Truth…"

"How do you know so much about the Bible?" Brandon asks, wondering.

"We study the stars, too, Brandon. God is not limited to just the boundaries of earth. We study all of humans' documents. Yet, the Bible, it is from Him," Dr. Drago says, adding, "I am sure Issac will concur."

"I thought you were against Issac's propositions of faith…" Brandon says.

"That was only a facade. With you, since you are my student, I have to be totally honest and open with you about the facts of the universe. Of course, I believe. It's how to connect with Him, for us, is where our exploration begins… Jesus gave you that connection."

"Did He give it to you, too?" Brandon asks.

"That's what I am trying to find out," Dr. Drago responds, adding, "Issac believes so. But, to me, I need to know more. The only book that mentions us is in the Book of Enoch and that didn't even make its way into the Bible. It was cut out. Maybe we were cut out, as well."

"My mom's probably looking for me. She wanted me to come home right after I picked up my homework," Brandon says, beginning to leave.

"So, where is it?" Dr. Drago asks, adding, "I need to continue with my exploration of the gathering of evidence."

"My homework?" Brandon responds.

"The entity, your Center, Brandon." Brandon glances over at a copper plated hatch in the corner. He appears shaken, quickly turns away.

"It's down there, isn't it? A powerful electromagnetic field..." Dr. Drago says, moving toward the hatch. "I felt it from the moment I can close to this dome..."

"You shouldn't go down there," Brandon says. Dr. Drago goes over and opens the hatch–BRIGHT BLUE LIGHT.

"Ah... The Nexus of the Metatron Cube, the genesis of life, Dark Matter's elusive electromagnetic field..."

Dr. Drago ShapeShifts into a reptilian and climbs down the shaft, a tunnel with a ladder, into the Blue Emanating Light as Brandon quickly runs out of the dome and toward his jeep, pulling out his fob and flicking on the headlights, staring the engine. He jumps in, drives off...

CHAPTER 10
Within a Reflection of Time

Crystal opens the door to the Ranch House with me right behind her. She lets me come in and slams the door, startling me.

"What was that all about?" I ask.

"Issac was right. The sheriff just took a report and blew us off. I think you told her too much. She didn't believe you. I mean, aliens? You're re-opening that bin again?" Crystal asks.

I look over to the grandfather clock and I noticed it stopped. "That's strange. That clock has never stopped." Suddenly, my concern for Brandon grows, noticing his folders tossed upon the dinging room table as I routinely toss my keys down upon it, rolling next to them.

"Are they Brandon's?" Crystal asks.

Stunned, I break from my *frozen* moment in time and frantically move toward the bottom of the stairs. I sense something is different, a vacuum of time engulfed in a memory leading to the top of the staircase as if being beamed upward into that light of the UFO, that night when I was trapped, *frozen in time.* I know my son's not up there, but I call out anyway. "Brandon!"

"I don't think he's up there," Crystal says, affirming my thoughts.

"That's so strange. I told him to come home right after school." I run up the stairs and burst into his room. Empty. I notice the telescope by the window, connecting me to that night...

Manhattan. 2001. I stand looking into the telescope in my sexy, revealing cowboy cheerleader's outfit. "Well, there's a dichotomy, Rosary beads and a sexy cheerleader outfit," Crystal laughed out, causing me to abruptly turn… facing myself from the past, a mirrored illusion, or so it seemed, within a distant, yet closely projected orb in time.

"Maria," Crystal says startling me, pulling me back into the present. "You look like you just saw a ghost."

"I saw myself, years ago, standing by my telescope back in our apartment in Manhattan," I reply, trying to solve the image of myself—what I saw. "Right there, by Brandon's window."

"You're just upset, about Brandon. Hey, maybe he's just hanging out with his friends, the girl he likes," Crystal says, gently, placing her hand on my shoulder as I continue to focus in on the telescope pointed out the window, adding, "Maybe he's exploring, or something…"

"He's grounded, remember?" I turn away from the telescope, adding, "You're right. I should have been a nun…"

I go back down the stairs with Crystal closely following and re-enter the dining room. I take out my phone and call Brandon. It rings, underneath the folders. Crystal lifts them up and hands be Brandon's phone. I look at his missed calls, *Tommy, Tommy, Brandi… Dr. Drago…* Shocked, my phone rings… I answer, put it on speaker as Crystal also appears concerned.

"Hello?" "Ms. Rivera?" "Yes."

"This is Julia. Mr. DeGenova's secretary. Well, I have good news. I finally found a tutor for Brandon, our music teacher volunteered…"

The grandfather clock rings out. I lower my phone, stare at Crystal, frozen again in time. "Then… who's Dr. Drago?" Crystal asks me as the clock stops ringing. I raise the phone.

"Thank you, Julia," I say in a forced calm voice. "I'll let him know." I hang up.

Look back up at the clock. It begins to move backward as I feel dizzy, being transformed into that of which I searched. Everything begins to blend, as gazing through a telescope with a large black hole forming—sucking everything in. I scream out from within, clasping my fingertips to the edges of the wooden window frame from 2001. "Crystal!" I cry out, feeling backed up to a wall. And yet, I go through it with the *bending of time…* I appear stunned, motionless, suspended in space as—*the clock ticks backwards…*

NYU Library, 2001. Julia sits close to me at the table with his hand upon my thigh. I notice the strange Fish Symbols on the Book before me in the past, remembering, with Julius's voice echoing through time…

"When the Big Bang occurred, there were particulate explosions in two directions… a mirror universe forming where time moves backwards and our's…

The grandfather clock sounds out again, awakening me from the past, propelling me into the future, the present of a chapter of my life with my two sons, appearing confused about the movement of time.

"Maria, are you alright?" Crystal asks, adding, "You look like you're somewhere else… an why is that clock moving backwards?"

"I dichotomy of universes," I say to myself with Crystal sympathetically listening. "A dichotomy of what?" Crystal responds as I focus in on the hands of the clock. "Universes. A black hole may be projecting string particulates… through space, time continuum, creating streams of quantum energy, projections, emanating from within a source into our dimensional time," I respond as if standing before a black hole in my life.

"Which means what, Einstein sister?"

"Two and three dimensional worlds are crossing through wave energy continuums upon vacuums in space," I echo out, repeating what Julius told me years ago at that table, caressing my leg, going higher upon my thigh, sending tingling sensations throughout me.

"So, what's that have to do with us?" Crystal crosses over time. I push Julius's hand away. "So… That's how they're getting here, from billions of light years away," I quiver out.

"Who?" Crystal asks, getting closer to me.

"Not who… they… them… Nephilim," I finally say, carrying these thoughts throughout the years, through all the years…

The lights in the dining room flicker in a Morse code Sequence.

"They're coming," I write with my pen in my journal, reading it aloud once written with a simple touch of a pen–*They're coming… I finally figured it out, those… those things, what they did to me,*" I thought to myself with a fearful stare and nod toward Crystal.

"Ugh… Them again? I need more pot so I can join you, in your… in your fantasy," Crystal says, attempting to dismiss our thoughts with a laugh and resolve of a hypothetical proposal of thought as to what happened back in 2001 on *the East Side.*

"It wasn't the bad pot, Crystal. It was all real… The dimensions of another universe crossed, changing me from an astrophysicist to a… that zombie soccer player… It was all real. She and I were just from another type of dimensional time."

"There are two of you?" Crystal says, turning toward the window of her soul.

"In a way. As time moves, so do we. Different versions of ourselves become prominent with each tick, moving, changing, growing, learning… experiencing what we create within our minds, within our souls…"

"So, a female zombie soccer player really went down on you, back then?"

"A version of me, yes. She was just in a parallel universe, the one where time moves backwards… forwards. It's kind of complicated. Still working on it, remembering, putting everything together…"

"Wow. You really researched… Why would dimensions cross?" Crystal asks.

"Because that's how they move, no just through space, but through dimensions of time." "Them? Nephilim?" Crystal says with a gasp.

"Yes. When they appear, from some kind of another dimensions, fourth, fifth; apparently they blend with our's in this third one, bringing glimpses of that other parallel universe, like a mirror… with them." I reply still somewhat confused, not knowing where my thoughts were coming from, the past, the present, the future?"

"A mirror?" Crystal asks, adding, "I am having trouble keeping up, sista from another universe. Where are you getting this all from? It's like your channeling some inner genius?

Maybe it's from Brandon…"

"Brandon," I whisper, grasping my concern, becoming frightened, clutching upon my Red Rosary Beads from long ago. "Dr. Drago…" I say louder, adding, "My son…"

"I was right about Drago…" Crystal says with a sarcastic grin and twist of an upper lip of concern. "Do you think he's alright?"

"Wait here," I simply say to Crystal, picking back up my keys and dashing out the door.

Crystal watches me through the window get into my monster truck and speed off.

As I drive down the road away from the ranch house, I begin to panic, crying. "My baby, my baby, Brandon," I repeat with each bump in the road, driving with one hand, wiping my tears away with the other. I remember what Brandon and I once talked about…

"Mom, why am I different?" Brandon, five-years-old asked me as he put together a train set, quickly, one Christmas beneath our tree."

"Why do you think you're different?" I asked, sitting down next to him as he turned on the train, moving down the tracks he aligned in various designs similar to those we found on the West Ridge, sending thoughts along the path of those tracks. "Why is he different?" I thought.

"Just because. I feel different," Brandon responded with Christian flying a toy jet by his father's side. "Am I?"

"Are you what?" I asked trying to just focus on the toys.

]   "Different," Brandon said, pushing down on the remote control box, moving the train faster around the tree with color lights turning on and off," beaming "on" and "off" in ticks of motion through time.

"Yes," I say aloud, in the present, driving down the road of our ranch in search of him. "You're different because you're a hybrid."

"What's a hybrid?" Brandon asked, in the past, while watching his train. "A cross between…" I paused as I glanced over at Christian and his father focusing in on the toy jet.

"An alien and a human," I say aloud, wiping away a tear, placing both hands on the wheel, gripping my determination to find my son, casting away my fear. Focusing on the grey cast mountains in the future–ahead.

Suddenly, several air force jeeps appear out of a haze, moving past me in the other direction, speeding toward our ranch house. *I pause–again, look back, and turn around.*

"Sometimes, to find the future, you have to go back into the past," I say as I grip the wheel tighter… turning around and driving back toward the ranch house, following the jeeps.

The grey mountains appear to move within my abrupt turn, my grip on the wheel, turning the world, blending the reflective, mirror images of itself from one dimension into another… Crystal moves toward the grandfather clock, in present time, the hands somehow moving back to its original position. She stares at it… wondering. She hears something– again–in my bedroom. She turns and goes down the hallway, opens the door.

Issac, stands by the side of my desk. He appears to be concerned– staring up at a BROKEN WINDOW PANE. He turns and looks at her as if looking through glass.

"Deja vu," Crystal says to herself, frozen within Issac's reflective stare at her, in a lustful forming way as Crystal adds, "A mirrored universe... Another version of Issac?"

"Must have been birds... or something," he says to her, standing frozen in the doorway. "Can I help you... Issac?" She asks, noticing my journal in Issac's hands.

"No. But, yes... I just came in here to look through Maria's journal. I am searching for where the others are," Issac says, gripping my journal, moving toward Crystal, unable to move.

"Searching for who?" Crystal says, shaking as he moves closer. Issac places my journal down upon my bed.

"Searching for what you are," Issac says with a smile, taking her by her hand and leading her toward the bed, sitting her down upon it, gently caressing her hair and guiding her back... Slowly taking off her clothes, Issac tosses them toward my desk with Crystal's panties landing on the back of my chair...

Crystal gazes at images of stars as Issac slides her, naked, further up the bed and gets atop of her. He pushes her arms over her head, gripping upon her wrists, kissing her on the side of her neck. Her legs begin to move apart, around him... She gasps... She turns... She screams...

In a full length mirror–The Reflective Image of a Grey Alien atop of her... She awakens from her fantasy in the mirror of another dimension of time.

"Found this on the floor when I came in. Just putting it back," Issac says, placing my journal back upon the desk with green unusual triangular scars on his forearm.

"What are you doing in here?" Crystal asks, confused. "Sorry. I'm looking for Maria. It's important. Need to talk to her, right away," he says manipulating the conversation toward a sense of urgency.

"She went to... find Brandon. Is there something I can help you with?"

"We found something up on the... East Ridge. I know Maria keeps a lot of books on that subject in here. So..." Issac says, trying to explain himself *again.*

"What do you think broke that glass, again?" Crystal asks, staring at the window. "Again?" Issac asks. "Yes again..." Crystal gasps out with the images within the mirror beginning to move, more forceful, more commanding within the other dimension of time with the grey alien moving atop of her, gazing upward toward the images of stars, blending with new found images of a reality… Crystal gasps louder… The horses in the gated area move in a gallop around the paddock, kicking and bucking as a gust of wind with rising dust swirls upward with the air force jeeps approaching… Crystal's head arches back as she momentarily glances upward into his slanted black eyes, feeling motionless, yet in a turmoil of a driving, pounding, turbulent wind, moving toward an unseen capitulating pulse of power within a distant time of *personage.*

CHAPTER 11
Greys, Draconians, and UFO's

Knock at the Front Door of the Ranch House… Crystal gathers her gasps as she suddenly finds herself stretched out naked upon the bed–alone. She turns, looks at herself in the mirror, sees Issac in a human form, standing in the doorway, staring at her. He turns away.

"Sorry, ma'am. I just wanted to let you know there are a couple of soldiers on the porch," Issac says with a tip of his cowboy hat, turning and walking away. Crystal looks at her clothes scattered about. She gets up and begins, quickly, putting them on with louder knocks on the door.

Disheveled, wrapping her blouse unbuttoned closer around her, Crystal tosses open the door. Two soldiers, air force, officers stand before her. "Yes…" Crystal begins to say as I pull up behind them in my monster truck. I jump out and approach them.

"Can I help you, gentlemen?" I ask, walking up on my porch.

"Ma'am. Sorry to come by, like this. But, we're just checking on your son," one of the officers says.

"You know something about Brandon?" I ask.

"No, ma'am. Your son, Christian. He was supposed to send us a report while on leave, involving an incident with an AUP. Is he here?" The other soldier asks.

"No. He was called back to the base a few days, ago," I reply, appearing more concerned.

Crystal opens the door all the way and goes onto the porch, standing next to me.

"Did he get back to the base?" Crystal asks them, buttoning the top of her blouse. "No, ma'am," they both reply, adding, "We were sent to find him."

"Come on, Crystal," I respond, leading her to my truck. "Get in!" I cry out as the soldiers watch us drive away. I pop the clutch into high-gear and peel out back down the same road.

"Deja vu," Crystal whispers, adding, "Now, we're looking for both your sons…" "What's going on? My husband vanishes, and now, Brandon and Christian," I say, driving faster, not realizing that a darkness of night was now upon us.

"Do you think you should slow down. You're going kind of fast," Crystal says, attempting to calm me down.

"What happened to you," I ask, noticing Crystal's blouse is buttoned unevenly. "It looks like you did a walk of shame…" Crystal begins undoing and re-buttoning her blouse.

"It was dark when I got dressed this morning. I didn't notice," Crystal tries to brush my comment aside.

"It was buttoned correctly when I left you. By the way, have you seen Issac?" I say with a slight smile, glancing over at her, then ahead. Crystal turns, looks out the glass, and answers, "I thought I did."

"What do you mean, 'You thought you did?' Did you see him back at the house or not?" Crystal turns and faces me. "Yes… and I let him kick it to me. He rode me like the stallions."

"Very funny," I respond, adding, "Well, if you do see him, tell him I need to clear out all the markings on the West Ridge. I want to move on from all of this. It's now affecting all of us. We need to break free from this darkness, right? Live normal lives?" Crystal touches my hand.

"It will workout. We'll find them," she says to me, "You'll see." "Did you really make love to Issac?" I ask, re-centering myself.

"To be honest, I am not sure… Maybe it was just a recurring fantasy. You know, like you're zombie soccer player…" Crystal says, taking her hand away.

"Oh, now I get it," I respond, moving ahead. "You had a couple of gummies." "Not really," Crystal responds with a raised eyebrow.

"Okay. Let's focus on where to find my sons. Any idea where they may be?" I ask, driving faster.

"I really think you should slow down. Should this thing be going this fast?" Crystal asks as my monster truck wobbles and rises up riding over small rocks. "I feel like we're about to take off," Crystal adds.

"No time to slow down. Do you see those fast moving clouds? It appears the dimensional fields are beginning to cross…" I respond, looking up.

"Maria… Did you have gummies?" Crystal asks in a serious tone. "No… Me?"

"Yes, you. You're sounding crazy, now. Dimensional Fields crossing, time stopping, reversing. Maybe we both should take deep breaths and… reverse our thoughts. I'll go first. What happened in your bedroom was just some kind of illusion, fantasy from our stress."

"You messed with Issac in my bedroom!" I cry out, adding, "In my bed!" "I told you, it was a fantasy," Crystal defensively replies.

"I am sure it was," I respond, adding, "Well, at least you're back at being you." "What's that supposed to mean?" Crystal asks, appearing to become angry.

"You know, the 'wild sister," I emphasize as Crystal gazes up at the fast moving clouds. "You became the 'wild sista, remember? What started all of this?" Crystal counters. "Started all of what?" I ask, pretending to not know.

"You opened that door to that parallel universe… through them," Crystal snips, adding, "And so what if I made love to Issac. I am single, right?"

"Okay, I'll slow down," I respond, slowing down the speed of my truck. "So, do you like him, Issac?"

"No… I am not sure," Crystal says, staring back out through the glass. "But, yes. In a way, yes… Don't worry. Everything will work out." Crystal looks back up at the sky. Briefly, she sees a fast moving UFO. "Do you see something," I ask noticing.

"I am not sure…" She responds, looking up and then back down—ahead toward the road. "Look out!" She cries out… I swerve my truck, seeing someone walking toward us—upon it.

With one swift turn, the grey-lined mountains hit me as a tornado coming out of nowhere.

Swirling, twisting, cascading upon me in a cold-centered-wave, I utter out… "It's Christian," slamming on the breaks, coming to an abrupt hard stop, sending plumes of dust around us, settling, clearing my thoughts—"It's Christian."

Walking in the center of the road, Christian staggers toward us, the beam lights of truck upon him as if a beam of light rising him up into *my night* with *They, Them, Us…*

I stop the truck, get out, and remain frozen in that night as Christian staggers toward us in the backdrop of my truck's beam of headlights emanating, as with my past, behind us. Breaking free from the past, I run to him. He collapses into my arms as I fall to my knees, cradling him.

Crystal stands in the distance, a shadow within the beaming lights. All I hear is her voice, "I'll call for an ambulance."

"No," I cry back, holding him tighter, his breaths rapid but strong, adding, "Let's figure out what happened, first. That sheriff has an attitude problem. BEAM OF HEADLIGHTS FLICKER. Crystal runs over to help. Christian appears confused, disoriented.

"We're close to our house. Let's just get him back. Once he's okay. I'll then go out, again, to search, to search for Brandon." Crystal helps me get Christian to his feet and walk him to truck, into those bright, beaming, flickering headlights…

Driving back, I stare at the road ahead, wondering, just wondering. Christian is breathing better, more deeper, calm. It doesn't look like he had been injured as he reclines comfortably in the backseat of my truck. His eyes are open but appear stunned, shaken in some way as if he had seen something… or rather, as I, experience something not of this world. Maybe I should have not began searching the stars, years ago, and just have kept my eyes on the road upon this planet, conforming to my role as a "wanna a be" scientist. Why did I step into Crystal's world and shift the balance of the entire dimensional plane between two parallel worlds and two parallel universes…

Why, why did I put on that cheerleader outfit? This question resonated within me over the past two decades, swirling around me as if I opened some kind of "black hole" doorway to… well, everyone is still trying to figure out what's in it, like me. What's inside me… Christian gasps, "Mom," awakening from whatever happened from him. "Are you alright?" I say to him, glancing at him sitting up, rising, in the backseat.

"Yes," Christian replies, bringing his hands to his head and noticing Crystal. "Aunt Crystal? What are you doing here?"

"I am helping your mom find you and…"

"And who?" Christian replies, adding, "What day is this?" "Thursday," I reply, continuing driving.

"The date, what's the date," he says more fervently.

"October third," Crystal replies, adding, "Why? What's going on? What happened to you?" Christian just stares ahead.

"Have I been missing?" He asks. "Yes," I reply.

"How long?" He responds, breaking out of his stare.

"Two weeks," I replies, adding, "You left two weeks ago."

"Two weeks! It seems like it was two hours!" Christian cries out, adding, "Who else is… missing?" Crystal and I glance at each other.

"Brandon…" Christian whispers out.

"Christian, it will be alright. We'll find him. He was supposed to come home. He did. He did come home. But, he went out again. Don't worry. We'll find him," I say attempting to calm myself down more so than Christian.

"Let me drive," Christian calls out. "Why?" I ask.

"Just let me drive. I drive faster than you," Christian gestures for me to pull the truck over as I begin to slow down. "No one drives my truck. Besides, we have to get you back home to make sure you're okay." "I am fine," Christian snips as I come to a stop and get out. Christian jumps up into the driver's seat and I duck into the back. "Don't worry. I am a fighter pilot, remember?" Christian turns the truck around and takes off…

Brandon flies across the desert, speeding off in his jeep. He hits a rock, overturns–Darkness, Lights. The jeep door is opened. Grey long fingers reach out to him from his upended jeep. Clasping upon him, they slide him out… The jeep explodes into flames.

On the West Ridge, inside the Dome, Dr. Drago opens the copper hatch and comes up out of the tunnel, cast in a blueish-tint glow. He notices Julius, from his expeditions in the Amazon, sitting by the control panel, wearing the old straw cowboy hat. Upon seeing him, Dr. Drago ShapeShifts back to a human form as the pulsating blue light visible in the tunnel beneath him.

He gets out, *closes the copper hatch,* and turns toward Julius, brushing himself seemingly as a matter of course off after ShapeShifting.

"Still digging inside tunnels, I see," Julius says with a swivel of his chair. "Well, it looks like our paths have crossed again. How did you find me, Julius?"

"I'm a good tracker... Did you know the fissures on that skull we found may have been a map? Oh, I also had that piece of metal analyzed." Julius arises from his seat and approaches the blue wall of the inner part of the Dome. "It appears to match... Interesting."

"What's interesting is that it took you that long to figure it out," Dr. Drago says, approaching and taking the piece of metal out of his hand."

"You knew?" Julius asks perplexed at Dr. Dragon's demeanor. "Of course, I did," Dr. Drago replies.

"Then why didn't you say anything?"

"I'm a teacher, Julius," Dr. Drago says with a smile. Holding up the blue metallic piece, he adds, "I like my students to discover for themselves the answers."

"Ah, a teacher, is that the manifest of your disguise, now?" Julius asks with returned slight mischievous smile as the inner part of the blue dome flashes on and off with various shades of translucent dimming lights.

"Qu'est-ce qui see passe?" Dr. Drago says placing down the metal by the control panel. "Yes, what's happening," Julius echoes with a humming sound rising around them.

"I think someone just took over the control panel," Dr. Drago replies with concern. "Who?" Julius asks, quieting himself.

"Them..." Dr. Drago ends.

"Aw, them," Julius adds going up to the control panel. Gazing at all the flashing lights in unison with the humming sound around them, Julius says, picking up the piece of metal, "It's a transmitter. Can send out radio waves at high frequencies.

Works on organic matter, merging brain cells to recollect erased memories from, well, you know."

"Very good, Julius. I think I'll put you in the advanced class. Would you like to... join us?"

"Us, they, them... I'll never join you, Draconian. I'm a tracker. Do you know what that

means?" Julius looks at Dr. Drago with an angered stare.

"Some of your friends did, once," Dr. Drago says, lowering his smile with a look of tightened discernment and returned show of fortitude.

"Zeta Reticulan are not our friends," Julius replies, adding, "I thought they were your's doctor?"

Dr. Drago turns away, moves toward a slanted peculiar shaped window of the Dome, gazes out toward the valley below. "We just collaborated, once, on that project at NYU. You must remember, Julius. Recollected memories? You've had that for quite a while, the metallic object, I mean. Didn't you say, you were studying biogenetic engineering or something in college?" Dr. Drago says, slightly turning back. "You remember, don't you Julius, if that's your real name. Why don't you just admit who you are, what you did to her, those many years ago on that campus. Gaze into the blue tint of your metallic memory."

Julius appears defensive as the flashing lights and humming sound stop. "You know why I participated in that genetics project, offering my sperm. You're the one, who decided to inject it in her, your subject. It wasn't out of a hypothetical scientific quest, but rather, in a Nordic driven consolidated effort to keep peace between your kind and the Greys. We are from a higher calling. We'll always be free… We'll never succumb to being your kinds' slaves."

Dr. Drago turns all the way around, faces Julius in a commanding stance and replies, "That's because we haven't made it to Erra, yet. The Reticulans we created serve a purpose, whereas, you Nordics, well, you never really interested us that much, only in a curious, perverse sort of way."

"Really? Even though us Nordics are creators of the universe? From a powerful realm, a part of Dark Matter? You know without our DNA that, that project at NYU would have never happened…" Julius pauses, glances over toward the copper hatch.

"You can take a look if you want, Nordic tracker. Maybe what you're ultimately searching for is down there," Dr Drago says, gesturing in a taunting manner.

"What I'm searching for is standing right in front of me," Julius banters back, still drawn toward the tunnel beneath the copper hatch.

"I understand. But, what's down there may surprise you, something that can change your life perhaps," Dr. Drago says in a tempting move of control again as Julius appears magnetized toward the tunnel. He nods, smiles, takes off his straw cowboy hat, places it down upon the control panel and gives in to the temptation, moving toward the closed copper plated hatch. On it, he sees the inscription, *Quis ut Deus.* "Who is like God?" Julius reads aloud, reaching down toward the hatch. "What's down there, Archangel Michael?"

"Another power. You'll find out. Go ahead, look…" Dr. Drago urges. "Find the Truth.

Seek and you will find; knock and the door will be opened to you. For everyone who asks receives; the one who seeks finds; and the one who knocks, the door will be opened."

Julius flings open the hatch, gazes down into the tunnel, into the pulsating blue light. "Ah, but what is Truth," he says, gazing into it. He hesitates, but turns around, steps down upon metallic steps, a steel ladder, and cautiously descends, climbing down, into a dark narrow tunnel, being engulfed within the blueish *warm* pulsating light... When he reaches the bottom of the ladder, he steps down into a heated room. Bright lights come on–small oval shaped illuminated shells upon the walls of a large bunker. He moves toward the center of the room–LOUD HUMMING SOUND, BECOMING LOUDER. He looks up–A BLUE AURA OF LIGHT, RESONATING–DARK MATTER. Julius raises his hand–IT BEGINS TO MELT. Frantically, he turns and climbs back up the metal latter that becomes hot with each clasp upon a metal rung.

THE HATCH IS CLOSED. LOCKED. POUNDING ON IT TO OPEN–HE SCREAMS.

Dr. Drago smiles and looks down at the copper hatch from above on the other side. "Alas, poor... Julius, I knew him well," Dr. Drago says, envisioning, examining the elongated skull.

Dr. Drago returns to the instrumental panel. The panel's lights come on, flicker, casting a reflection upon him. He sits down in the swivel chair amidst Julius's anguished screams and put on the straw cowboy hat. His eye ShapeShift to a REPTILIAN YELLOW–INVERTED PUPILS. He places his hands, his coiled reptilian morphing skin upon the flickering green lights. He begins maneuvering them with a rising humming sound overcoming Julius's fading screams. "Now... to help Brandon capture his shooting star..."

CHAPTER 12

Cheerleaders, a Swing, and A Light

Red Rock High School. The football stadium lights come on as Brandi and other cheerleaders make their way out onto the center of the field, wearing striped school color tights. One cheerleader turns toward Brandi and asks, "So."

"So, what?" Brandi replies.

"Did you decide, yet about who you are going to the prom with? That Brandon is really cute, a little strange, but cute…" Brandi looks up. She sees Rocco coming toward them at the center of the field.

"Well, look who it is," the cheerleader says to Brandi.

Brandi turns and says, "I'll be right back. You guys can started without me." Brandi walks away toward Rocco, intercepting him before he got to the center of the field with the other cheerleaders. The cheerleaders, beginning to practice, glance over at them with concern.

Rocco, towering over Brandi, wearing his #77 football jersey, appears angry. "So, have you decided, yet? You're going to the prom with me, right? I mean, you are still my girl."

Brandi places her hands upon Rocco's chest. "Rocco… I think we need a break. "It's because of that Brandon, isn't it?" Rocco brushes her hands away, adding, "I'm going to break his face…"

"See, this is what I mean. You're always getting angry. Look, just give me space," Brandi turns her back on Rocco and begins walking back toward the group of cheerleaders at the center of the field–as Rocco appears ready to explode–his eyes turning yellow with inverted pupils…

"There he is!" Christian cries out, seeing Brandon's overturned inflamed jeep. Christian comes to an abrupt stop, tail spinning the monster truck. Crystal and I jump out, flinging their doors open, and run toward the flames. "Brandon!" I cry out. Christian follows.

I find Brandon sitting on the ground, his arms folded around his knees–silent. "Brandon, are you alright?" I ask as he stares ahead listlessly, appearing trapped somewhere in the past.

"Mom?" I finally says to me with all of us crouched down around him. I hug him. "Come on, bro. Let's get you home," Christian says, helping him up and back toward the truck. As they get in, I glance back to the grey lined mountains. I see an orb, a bright oval shaped object moving in rectangular patterns throughout the sky. It appears, as if, it's moving toward the direction of the high school…

When they enter the ranch house, Christian helps Brandon into the dining room and sit's him down in a chair by the dining room table. "Are you sure you're alright, bro?" He asks.

"Yes, I'm fine," Brandon replies, adding. "What happened?" I ask, going up to his side.

"I was driving my jeep and out of nowhere, it turns over," Brandon says, looking up, adding, "then, then this weird hand reached out to me and pulled me out."

The front door of the ranch house opens. Issac enters. "What's going on… Christian?" "Yes, Issac. It's me. I'm back," Christian says, giving Issac a stare.

"Christian, what happened to you?" I ask, interrupting the stare in an attempt to break the ice of discontent beginning to fill the room. The Welcome Home sign falls.

Christian turns away from Issac, touches Brandon's shoulder and replies, "I'm really not sure. I must have been in some kind of, well, car accident like Brandon. One minute, I was in the back seat, heading toward the base, and the next minute I saw a strange oncoming headlight… It looked like it was coming from the sky." Christian picks up the sign, places it down on the side of the table. "Are you sure, two weeks have past? It still seems like two hours…" Christian says as he appears suddenly distant, in a way, disoriented, now staring at the grandfather clock…

Christian is led down a metallic hallway and into a cockpit of a UFO. An alien pilot turns toward him–smiles–The alien he saw through the window flying above the Baltic Sea…

Christian awakens, turns away from the clock, and looks at me. "Sorry, mom. I must have just hit my head in my car accident, got thrown from the car or something, walked across the desert when you found me. But, it's okay, mom. I'm home, now."

"Well, it looks like you have both your sons home, now, Maria," Crystal says. "See, everything worked out." Issac nods, begins to leave.

"Issac, can I talk to you upstairs? I think you know what it's about," Christian says, taking his hand off Brandon's shoulder, giving Issac a stern determined look. Issac, hesitantly, nods again. Christian follows Issac up the stairs as Brandon continues to gather himself. The grandfather clock strikes a mysterious tone. Crystal and I look at each other—then over at the staircase. I hand Brandon back his phone. He looks at it—Missed Call—BRANDI...

Red Rock High School. Football Stadium. The cheerleaders are finishing up practice at the center of the football field with the bright lights of the stadium beaming down upon them.

"Great practice, everyone!" Brandi cries out.

The cheerleaders gather up their cheerleading props and then begin to exit the field, together. Brandi walks alongside the other cheerleader, who asked about the prom. "You know what I think?" The cheerleader says.

"About what?" Brandi replies as they exit the stadium.

"I think you should go to the prom with Brandon," the cheerleader replies.

"We'll see," Brandi responds, pausing. She looks into her backpack, appearing upset. "What's the matter?"

"I forgot my phone. Go ahead. I'll catch up to you guys," Brandi says, turning and walking back inside the stadium.

"Do you want me to go with you!" The cheerleader cries out to her. "That's okay... I'll be fine! Really, just go ahead!" Brandi cries back.

The cheerleader watches with concern as Brandi goes back into the stadium, alone. She looks up, sees a bright light—an oval orb.

Brandi makes her way, again, back to the center of the field. She finds her phone she dropped and picks it up—The stadium's lights go out, leaving her completing in the dark.

"What the..." she says to herself. She shines the light on her phone. But, it's not enough to overcome the darkness that suddenly fell upon her, surrounding her, with a coldness, a wind.

A bright light appears hovering above her. She attempts to look up into this blinding light.

Feeling a stronger wind, as if the object was descending upon her—fearful, she runs… as the object follows her, continuing to hover, getting brighter, closer…

"Oh, my God… Oh, my God!" Brandi cries out, dropping her backpack, running faster while clasping upon her phone. She runs across the field, through the stadium. She comes to a rickety meshed wire fence surrounding an abandoned playground. Frantically, she pushes her way through a small opening, breaking free into the playground, bumping into playground equipment with the light of the object descending upon her… lighting up the darkness.

Brandi clutches upon a swing, dangling from two rusted iron linked chains as she sees a beam of light begin to encapsulate her. "Brandon!" She shocks herself calling out, dropping her phone, her hands breaking free from the swing, being pulled upward into a cyclone of swirling wind and light…

Emerging from hiding behind the playground, in a residue of befallen darkness, is the cheerleader, her friend, clasping upon Brandi's backpack—Frozen in fear as if within an icicle of reflecting time, Brandi rises up into a tunnel of light… disappearing into the UFO that flies off, vertically becoming absorbed in a darkness, into shadowy images, swaying back and forth, *like the swing,* with the night… Empty. Silence. A light comes on Brandi's phone, ringing on the rubber pellets of the playground beneath the swing *moving back and forth* in a lowering wind— BRANDON.

Brandon hangs up and places his phone down upon the dining room table. He looks up at Crystal and me. "I'm going to go see what they're doing," he says to me as he heads to the stairs.

"Okay, Brandon," I reply back to him, adding, "I'm glad you're okay," not wanting to press him on really what happened and about Dr. Drago. Brandon responds with a simple nod and heads up the stairs.

Confused, shaken, I sit down at the dining room table, staring at the clock, trying to analyze and come to a conclusion as to what had occurred this bizarre night with both my sons. Crystal, sensing and understanding that I was in my *astronomical empirical analysis data mode,* says, "I'll let you figure all of this out, Einstein sista."

She disappears down the hallway and into the kitchen as I begin wondering, just wondering… staring at the clock, reflecting about the movement of time, the relation to space, and about what really happened that night, back on *the West Side* of our Manhattan apartment in my sexy cheerleading outfit in which I succumbed to my passions of wanting to be something different, something attractive, something powerful in a sensual, magnetic resonating, pulsating, and emanating way. Yet, what did I ultimately attract? I turn away from fearful thoughts and gaze out the dining room window. I see the horses galloping about in the light of a night's sky. I think about my father, how he said to always choose wisely because that is what you will become. He guides me down off the horse as a child, takes me by the hand, and walks off with through time. What have I become? Crystal slams downs a couple of full bottles of wine before me…

CHAPTER 13

Symbol of a Fish, Civilizations of Watchers, a Grey

When Brandon enters his bedroom, he sees Christian has Issac pinned up against the bedroom wall. "For the last time, tell me where you're from! Who sent you!" Christian cries out.

"Christian, what are you doing?" Brandon asks, attempting to get between them and break it up. "Stay back, Brandon," Christian says, pushing Brandon away, adding, "He knows what I'm doing. Right Issac?" Christian says, backing off as Issac stays against the wall.

"No one sent me," Issac responds, attempting not to ShapeShift, shaking…

"Okay, look. I may have just spent a couple of weeks in some Reptilian's UFO getting probed… So, for the last time, tell me where you're from! Who sent you!"

"No one sent me," Issac echoes, again, his hand beginning to ShapeShift; long grey fingers, elongating with his eyes becoming slanted and black… Christian grabs in by his throat.

"Come on, let him go," Brandon calls out, noticing Issac's elongating grey alien fingers. Brandon pulls Christian away. Issac bends over, coughing, slowing rising, ShapeShifting into his Zeta Reticulum form, casting a reflection within a semi-full length mirror hanging on the slightly open, ajar bedroom door. Christian gives an affirmative nod and smile toward Brandon.

"Yes, Brandon," Issac's an alien. Christian slams the door all the way shut. He sees a light emanating from Issac's room from his apartment, through Brandon's bedroom window and upon the door before them. Christian turns, places his hands upon the symbols formed by the light. "Do you see these symbols, Brandon?"

Issac stands in semi-full length alien form. Looking at Issac, Brandon responds, "Yes. I noticed them before. Wondered what they were, what they meant." Brandon turns to Christian.

"Why don't you tell him, Issac the alien?" Christian says, gesturing with his fist.

Issac moves toward the symbols, his head forming around his slanted black eyes. He places his long grey fingers upon the symbols, fully transforming, as if calculating the angles.

"Can he read my mind?" Brandon asks Christian.

"Yes. So, don't think of anything weird," Christian replies.

"Hello. I'm here in the room," Issac replies, further examining the symbols, adding, "And, yes, I can read your thoughts. It's not weird, me being an alien. A lot of people are… Versica Piscis. "

"Versica Piscis, the true design of the universe, Brandon," Christian says, placing his hand atop Issac's alien hand, adding, "We're all a part of it, humans and… aliens."

Issac turns, bringing down his hand along with Christian's, and says ShapeShifting back to his human form, "This symbol, Brandon, the Bladder of the Fist, is found in religions and all type of architecture throughout history with various writings on walls, signs, messages. Yet, only a few take the time to care to see… as time, throughout history, moves on with things in the background, well, that many just don't understand."

"Issac the alien is right. The symbol of the Fist represents something, the crossing of heaven within another dimension and… earth," Christians says, staring at Issac turning back. Christian turns toward Brandon, appearing shocked.

"What's the matter with you?" Christian asks him.

"What's a matter with me? I just found out our ranch hand is an alien and somehow you know a lot more than…"

"A fighter pilot?" Christian says, placing his hand on his brother's shoulder. Brandon nods. "That's because I'm more than a fighter pilot." Christian turns toward Issac.

"You know, don't you, Issac?" Issac nods. "I know what you are. Why don't you tell your brother? Everything is connected, Brandon. Just like with the show Ancient Aliens. Christian iconography from the time that Jesus told his disciples to cast their net into the sea where they pulled exactly one hundred and fifty-three fishes out of the *right side...*

"I don't understand. What are you, bro?" Brandon asks Christian, adding, "What does one hundred and fifty-three mean?"

Christian pauses, looking at Issac. "You see, Brandon, Vesica Piscis can be divided into four equal right triangles whose height and width are expressed in the ratio 265:153."

"Who are you?" Brandon asks his brother, appearing confused, stunned.

"Thus, the number one hundred and fifty-three holds a special significance in the Book of John. The division of 265:153 is condensed to 1.73203 and the closest square root to number...

3. Hence, the square root of 3–is called, THE MEASURE OF THE FISH. "Are you an alien, Christian?" Brandon asks, measured.

"I'm telling all of this to you for a reason, Brandon. Don't worry what I am. You must understand, more importantly, who you are... many of us are depending on it, many from not on this planet. You're connected, Brandon," Christian says, sympathetically.

"To what? To who?" Brandon asks, adding, "Tell me."

"The Measure of the Fish has been a connected to cultures and civilizations for over a couple thousand years," Issac says, interrupting Christian's pause, adding, "In Orthodox Christianity, Vesica Piscis was found in the religious depictions of Jesus. During the Gothic period, the arches, windows, vaults, and porches of cathedrals were based on Viscia Piscis geometry. They, them, created the universe, some believe. Yet, there's a force outside what they created more powerful than... them, that enabled *them* to create it. And now..."

"And now what?" Christian asks as he and Brandon turn Issac.

"They're all coming here, to this ranch in Arizona. Each circle they marked on both the West and East sides represents a galaxy, a designation of a home to each alien civilization," Issac responds, turning toward Christian. "I know what you are."

Brandon walks up to the markings on his door. "Why do those lines triangulate like that?" "They're aligned to locations of a high-yield energy source... Did you ever go into my room?" Christian asks Brandon. "I have," Issac replies.

"I am sure you did. Is that how you know who I am?" Christian responds. "And other discoveries," Issac simply replies with a smile.

"No. I never went into your room, Christian. You always told me not to, remember?" Brandon finally responds, adding, "What's in there?"

"I've been meaning to tell you something, for a while, now…" Christian says.

Strong wind. Weathervane spinning atop the house. The symbols on the door fade.

Half of the bottle of the *second wine bottle* is empty as Crystal and I slug down shots from our fancy wine glasses, sitting at the dining room table with *the other bottle*–empty.

"I'm staring to feel it," I say, twirling the wine in my glass.

"This wine is expensive. A patient gave it to me, said it was a hundred dollar bottle of some kind of special wine," Crystal responds with a sip.

"Why are you sipping it, now? You were just slugging it a minute ago," I say with a smile. "Because… I'm a lady." "You're not a lady." "Okay, whore sista… or did you forget."

I put down my glass, stare at my friend, for so many years and wonder. "I didn't forget." "I know," Crystal responds, placing her glass down next to mine. "So, you have both

your sons back, together under one roof. Now what?" "I am not sure. I am starting to feel…"

"The wine?"

"No. Something else," I say, glancing up at the grandfather clock. It appears to be moving backwards. "Time is moving backward? The dimensional portal is opening?"

"Okay, now you're freaking me out. I have no idea what you're talking about or imagining," Crystal says, picking back up her wine glass and drinking the remnants of wine, the remnants of her thoughts matching mind from that night of the light… *they, them…*

"They're coming," I say out loud, calmly, with my frozen look through time, clasping upon my red Rosary beads, causing Crystal to whisper, "Maria…" and drop her glass.

"I'm not ready for this, again," Crystal says, trying to mop up the spilled wine. She takes the left over wine and drinks it directly from the bottle. Slamming down the bottle on the dining room table, she echoes, with her hands shaking, "I'm not ready for this, again… Not like this, anyway."

Crystal reaches into her pocket and takes out gummy bears, green, purple, and blue.

"What are they?" I ask, knowing.

"You know what they are," Crystal replies, standing over me, adding, "Go ahead. Take one." I stand up. "There is absolutely no way I am going to take any of your pot, again."

"I think after all these years, all the running away, it's..." Crystal says, reaching out the gummy bears toward me.

"It's... what?" I ask, knowing.

"It's time we re-open that bin," Crystal says. "Let's take a trip back into the past and see what really happened, sista from another universe. You had courage once to walk out that door." I hesitantly nod, the smile.

"Let's do it," I add with a wider smile. It's time..." We both pop a handful of gummy bears in our mouths... and for some bizarre reason, we laugh, somehow, we laugh... as we did dancing in our underwear in that apartment on *the West Side*–those many years ago...

I punch open a trap door to the attic with a burst of laughter while standing atop an old wooden rickety ladder with Crystal behind me, taking slugs of the remaining bottle of wine, building her own courage driven by images of green, purple, and blue... in the palm of her hand.

"Be careful, wild sista from another universe," she cries up to me.

I make it up through the trap door and into the attic. I turn, reach back down and help pull Crystal up into the attic, the doorway to the past, a quest in time to find answers, echoing within. Finding a single light bulb suspended from the ceiling, I reach up and pull on a chain–LIGHT. Instead of a golden realm of answers with glittery mystical adornments; before us, lay cobwebs, a partially completed floor, disheveled insulation, and dust, nothing like what I had imagined being up here for all these years.

"So is this the Yellow Brick Road to Oz you imagined?" I ask Crystal.

"It will be," Crystal responds, gesturing toward the corner of the attic in the shadows, adding, "Look."

"Seek and you shall find..." I whisper, seeing it, what had been echoing within us throughout time–THE BIN, the KEY to all of our secrets, our past passions, and personas. Everything, symbolized by various outfits, sexy and very sexy were ALL in that, that BIN.

Christian searches in his closet with Brandon and Issac standing outside the closet behind him. "What are you looking for?" Brandon asks, peering in.

"My past," Christian says, adding, "What I had to tell you."

"I found it," Christian says, punching in a code in on a strange appearing panel and turning on a switch. A red light becomes visible and hums on his bedroom wall by a bookshelf as Christian emerges from the closet. The bookshelf begins to move to the side exposing a large vault of unusual appearing weapons.

"You have weapons? In your bedroom?" Brandon asks, adding, "Does mom know?"

"I have them everywhere. I have been waiting for this moment," Christian says, turning and facing Brandon. "I'm part of an elite team that my own commanders in the air force don't even know about. I've been trained to fight…"

"Who?" Brandon asks.

Christian begins gathering up the weapons. He turns back and stares at Issac. "Aliens." Issac takes a step back and says, "I know what you are. We call you, Indagatrix."

"What does that mean?" Brandon asks.

"Tracker," Christian responds grabbing hold of an old duffle bag and placing the weapons into it. "Actually, you're only half right. The term is Indagatrix veritatis, is the proper name."

"Ah, Searcher of Truth…" Issac responds, adding, "I like that… Indagatrix veritatis." "Our mission, Brandon, is to locate Grey's, like Issac here. The Grey's are friendly. The Reptilians, not so much. They look like us as, well, like we look at insects."

"How did you escape? The Reptilians usually eat the brains of humans," Issac says to Christian as he zips up the duffle bag.

"They let me escape. Probably put a tracking device in me to get to… You, bro. Didn't mom ever tell you…" Christian says, standing up and tossing the duffle bag over his shoulder.

"Tell me what?" Brandon asks.

Christian takes hold of his arm. Turns it over–tattoo–*IBRIDA*.

"Hybrid," Issac says, glancing over at the open vault with a few weapons left. "Do you mind?" Issac asks, Christian.

"Please, the more help, the better," Christian says with an affirmative nod.

Christian with his duffle bag over his shoulder, Issac with another duffle bag over his shoulder, and Brandon walk defiantly toward the monster truck outside the ranch house.

"Let's Rock "N" Roll," Christian says to them…

CHAPTER 14

The Past, the Present, the Bin

In the attic, Crystal and I stare at the bin, wondering. "Well, are we going to go over there and open it?" Crystal asks with a chuckle, adding, "I'm so stoned. You?

I turn on my phone, unknowingly clasped in my hand all this time, and shine it through the Dark Shadows of a distant time, resonating as if a heartbeat within the bin in the corner, draped in cobwebs of motionless reality captured beneath wooden beams of rusted thoughts vibrating with an unseen echo from the past, as if a radio signal, cast out from some distant planet in another parallel universe, another version of… me.

"Hey, sista from another universe, are we going to open it?" Crystal asks again as I point my flashlight on my phone toward the awaiting BIN, luring us as if some man siren at sea.

"I feel like we've been up here for years, standing here, like this, waiting…" Crystal says. "We haven't been up here for years, Crystal. We've been living our lives," I say, adding,

"Okay, you're right. I'm really feeling those gummy bears."

"How do you know it's not the wine?" Crystal replies, adding, "You know, a part of us have been up here for a very long time. You know, we have a lot of what do the experts call it, unresolved issues, and all of them are in that BIN.

"That's just the wine talking or, the gummy bears, not sure which one," I say, adding, "Brandon may be right, it's not the wine or the gummy bears, it's both. They're both connected."

"What in the world are you talking about?" Crystal asks as we move arm in arm toward the bin. "Well… I mean, it's not Faith and Science separate, it's Faith and Science together. For centuries people have viewed Science as discounting, disproving God. But, now, Science proves God, proves Faith…"

"Wow, these are some powerful gummy bears," Crystal says as we stand before our past, that moment in time, that BIN. "So, the wine symbolizes Faith and the gummy bears symbolize Science."

"Exactly," I respond, gazing down at the BIN, our past and future Destinies.

"Are you going to open it?" Crystal asks as I feel myself being sucked, pulled out that window of that night long ago by they, them, afraid to take that step back into the past.

"I'm not sure," I respond, feeling as if my red Rosary beads were in my hand.

"If you don't open it, then we just wasted a couple hundred dollars of wine and, not to mention, very strong gummy bears…" Crystal says, signaling me to get down and open it.

"I don't want to waste gummy bears…" I simply say as I crotch down before the BIN. "You mean, you don't want to waste Science," Crystal says with a laugh.

"I don't want to waste Faith," I say as I look at a thick layer of dust with images of words written atop the cover of the BIN. I shine my phone upon it–*Quis ut Deus.*

"What does Quis ut Deus mean?" Crystal asks, appearing drawn to the BIN.

"Let's find out," I reply, tossing open the BIN, reopening the past… Reaching in, as if reaching into my soul, I find and pull out my old sexy cheerleading outfit. I smile, reflecting upon an image of a past persona I treasured, feared, and felt torn about in terms of my actions,

my growth, and my own cast-doubt morality over which direction of space I should have pointed my telescope at in a heartfelt moment to explore the universe and what was inside myself.

"Here's your's," I add, taking out Crystal's old alien costume. I hand it to her as if I had just found a treasure in a treasure chest buried far deep beneath the sand.

"Ah, my alien costume," Crystal responds, taking it and holding it to her chest, adding, noticing, "I wonder why it has blood on it…"

"Are you going to put it on?" I ask with a smile, adding, "I think you should put it on.

See if it fits. Maybe it will awaken memories..."

"I'll put on mine if you put on your's, whore sista," Crystal responds, gesturing toward my sexy cheerleading outfit. See if it still fits," she says with a smile, adding, "Come on, you know you want to... Follow the feeling of the gummy bears."

"You mean, the wine," I say with a returned smile, beginning to take off my clothes with an impromptu seductive, sexy dance...

Crystal laughs out. "You're stripping?" She takes my phone and begins recording it. "Don't worry, I won't post it. Just trying to capture the *wild sista* from the past... Go girl."

"I'm trying to reenact that night... Maybe it will help me remember," I say, suddenly hearing music emanating from the past. Smoke filling the room. The window open before me...

Crystal looks into the BIN. She finds an old CD and a battery operated CD player. She pops it in, hits play. MUSIC. "Let's take a ride in your hoochie outfit time capsule, whore..."

I begin dancing more seductively, twisting and turning, feeling two worlds through music collide, imagining smoke of merging time fill the room... in my pink thong.... *Remembering...*

"Go Maria... Go Maria!" Crystal's words echo from the darkness of the attic, throwing me back through a tunnel of time encapsulated by my sensual *alternative universe self...* capitulated within beats of imagined, crossing realms of music–scattered memories rising through pieces of sand slipping through my fingertips, clasped upon a pen–writing, in my journal... They *Grey* lined mountains before me... *I surrender to my thoughts... as I write...*

I'll never forget. But, I'll never remember, I keep telling myself within the shadow-cast images of my soul as I continue to gaze out toward an unusual sun, pushing it back even past my darkest thoughts of the most secret part of my mind, the secret yearning passions within me...

The Grandfather Clock Strikes Beats of Tones–Casting Me Back Through Time...

The green haired Zombie woman reached down and, gently, guided me to my feet. After taking off my cowboy hat and football jersey, she turned me around and pushed me up against a post. I shook, that weird tingle returning, exploding, as she began caressing me – sliding down my legs, my pink thong panty to my ankles… I felt recaptured… tied again to the mast of a ship. The tights fell from my hands as I deeply gasped, feeling her long fingers move up my legs… closing my eyes…

Fall 2001. "Go, Maria! Shake it, sista!" With my eyes closed, I kept dancing, feeling warmth of a subtle sudden breeze coming in, awakening those tingles up and down my spine from when I saw him, the man with the grey-yellow eyes, feeling his touch upon my cheek…

BRIGHT LIGHTS. Humanlike small figures with smooth grey color skin, enlarged elongated heads, and slanted eyes emerged from the smoke of pot permeating the room. Crystal noticed them first, appearing shocked, fearful, pointing toward them with her mouth agape. "Maria," Chrystal struggled to whisper to as if frozen in silence.

My eyes opened in shock. I tried to call out but my screams became silent as they took hold of me, grabbing me from around my waist behind, feeling their long grey fingers around me and the cast out images of their dark slanted eyes… as they pulled me back toward the window. I couldn't break free as I attempted to scream out louder within a befalling silence with Crystal reaching out toward me, seemingly from another dimension as they yanked me with more of a solitude of force out the open window and upward into bright hovering lights. Crystal's cries grew faint as silence grew around me, except for small echoes of sounds of traffic in the city echoing in the streets below.

"Maria!" Crystal's voice grew distant in her dimension, drowned out by the city traffic below while she gazed up in shock, staring out the open window as I was pulled upward by an unknown force, seemingly a reverse gravitational pull, toward a hovering elongated lighted disk. I vanished into a darkened void, feeling coldness upon my skin, tingling with a strange sensation as bits of less air centered upon me, causing me to gag, flowing as sand from a glass into my lungs, as I gasped for air within a vacuum of complete silence. Within a twirling tunnel of darkness. I found myself floating upward toward an opening, a light, as I was frozen in fear, unable to move, in a horizontal position, face-up, rising… and rising, further and further away from our apartment building far below. I closed my eyes, as if I had entered a dream, hoping with each struggled breath that I would awaken safely in my bed… Crystal was curled up in a fetal position in the corner, appearing catatonic, twirling her hair… the rap music still sounding out, the smoke escaping out the open window with the music fading, upward toward a star filled sky draped in an unseen invasion of a befallen stillness…

Floating in the reticence of darkness, feeling like I was submerged in water, I continued to be elevated in my forced prone position, my arms outstretched by my side, upward, through an intense crepuscule cyclone of a warped spinning tunnel. Finally, once above the surface, I gasped out the residue of sand and opened my eyes, taking deep breaths as I could breath again, and again. I had been lifted up into something that appeared to be some kind of metallic spaceship.

The Greys, who I discovered had captured me, quickly, stood me up and hurriedly guided me down a long hallway with unusual lights upon the ship's internal metallic walls. A few of the Greys appeared to be piloting the ship with several, appearing to be like robots, stood still, motionless, aligning the hallway; emotionless, unmoving, without expression, seemingly disinterested in me being led in strong grips by my arms as a captive down their futuristic, out of this world, appearing guarded hallway.

When I entered the room, it seem sterile, white, cold, like an operating room. There were aliens standing by a long metallic table with straps. They had metallic appearing instruments in their long Grey fingers. Surprised, I noticed people behind them, sitting in the background, as if about to watch a performance, a show, with them encircling the table, the stage.

Two of the Grey's led me over to the table while the others took their place next to what appeared to be alien doctors, surgeons. Two had surgical masks on. I broke free of my frozen fear and began to shake uncontrollably as they laid me on the table as if I was a captured specimen, tying me me down, totally naked, spread eagle upon the coldness of the metallic table.

A tall REPTILIAN ALIEN, with GREY-YELLOW EYES, stood over me as if I knew him. Slowly, he got on top of me… As I felt him enter me, my body shook in a sensual, tingling explosive exhilaration as I gazed upward, looking around me at the aliens and humans centered behind three images of the future, removing their surgical masks. I became shocked, stunned, churning at their gazes down upon me. There they were, my future, DR. DRAGO, and… ISSAC. They stared down at me in a listless, chilling science driven genetic haze, using me for an alien collaboration of a quantum multi-species design comprised of science, and yet, something else happened… God stepped in and gave me a son, a beautiful boy, with a wondrous–amazing spiritual soul… Filled with love, the most powerful force in the universe…

The chimes of the clock… Present Day. Brandon gazes out the truck's window toward the grey lined mountains with Christian driving my monster truck. Issac sits in the back, watching Brandon's look as if waiting for something, to witness Brandon's transformation and realization as to who he is…

"You know, mom is going to be really mad that you stole her truck," Brandon says, turning toward Christian.

"It's okay. We're on a mission to hunt aliens, those reptilians. She'll understand," Christian responds, pushing his foot further down on the accelerator.

"Doesn't matter. She'll still get mad. You know how she is. This truck is very special to her. Dad gave her this truck," Brandon says clarifying.

Christian lets up on the gas, slowing down. "I know," Christian says, calming. "What happened to your father?" Issac asks.

"I thought you would know," Christian says, glancing into the back seat.

"No. I don't. None of us do," Issac responds, adding, "I heard about him, though." "Let's just focus on our mission," Christian says, trying to change the subject, noticing Brandon is getting upset.

"It's your mission, bro," Brandon says, adding, "I just want to see Brandi. Make sure she's okay…" Brandon's phone beeps. A text from Tommy.

Tommy–*hey, they took your girl*

Brandon–*what! who???*

Tommy–*our school mascot. one of the cheerleaders saw it. rounding everyone up* Brandon appears shocked. He let's his phone slip to the truck's floor from his hand. "What happened, bro? You alright?" Christian asks.

Brandon turns to Christian, then back toward Issac. "They took Brandi."

"Well, it looks like our missions crossed. Don't worry. We'll get her back," Christian says adjusting his phone to a song, connecting it to the Blue Tooth of the truck.

"They're up to something. Reptilians are very calculated. There must be a reason they took… Brandi. Where did you meet her, Brandon?" Issac asks from the back, leaning in.

"At school. She's a student… I don't want my girlfriend's brains to be eaten," Brandon cries out. "I'm picking up the speed. I sense something's happening up on the West Ridge…" Christian says, shifting into a higher gear, pressing down on the accelerator as Brandon picks up his phone from the floor, glances at it… Tommy–*where do you want to meet?* Begins to text -

Brandon–*west ridge of my ranch… everything's going down up there. Call the calvary, bring the heat…* Tommy–*Roger that…*

"Did mom every tell you, Brandon?" Christian asks, focusing on picking up speed.

"Tell me what?" Brandon responds, still upset, glancing out the window. "About…" Christian reaches over and turns over his arm— *IBRIDA.* "About this. Issac, instead of just staring at him, do you want to tell him?

"Brandon," Issac begins to say, "IBRIDA means…"

"Hybrid. I know. Don't you think I'd look it up by now. It's Latin and I am top of my class, you know, honors program," Brandon replies back.

"So, you know? That you're an alien hybrid?" Christian replies acting surprised. "An alien hybrid! I thought it just meant to be environmentally conscious," Brandon

staring at the mark on his arm, adding, "Are you a hybrid?" "No. But, you are. Mom was…" Christian begins to say.

"Let's just say you're unique," Issac interrupts, adding, "There are unique people in the world and you're one of them, a gift, of sorts.

"A gift?" Brandon gazes back out the window, "What kind of gift?"

"You're a human-alien-alien-alien hybrid, three types of alien DNA, bro," Christian says, playing a song from Woodstock Music Festival in the 60's–turning up the music…

"The best music, ever, the 60's, Dylan, Franklin, Hendrix…" Christian says, nodding his head to the music from Woodstock.

"You steal mom's truck. You tell me I'm a triple alien hybrid and now you're listening to music from decades ago? You know what I think?" Brandon says, becoming angry.

"What?" Tim asks, singing.

"You're the one who's the alien," Brandon says, covering up the mark on his arm. "Touche'," Issac relies in the back.

"So, where are we going, again?" Brandon asks.

"The West Ridge, bro," Christian says, looking up at the sky, seeing UFO's passing quickly high above them, overhead. "I'm right. Our version of Woodstock. Everyone, everything is converging up there... from all parts of our Galaxy... Right, Issac?"

SIXTIES MUSIC–WOODSTOCK–SLY AND THE FAMILY STONE "HIGHER."

"Let's fly, little brother," Christian says, pushing the accelerator to the floor and taking off at a HIGH speed across the open desert off road.

"I want to take you higher..." Christian sings to the music.

"I want to take you higher... I want to take you higher, gon' be alright... Let me take you higher, yeah, yeah, yeah, Higher, ooh, higher..." Issac sings out loudly in tune in the backseat to the music.

Christian pauses. Christian and Brandon look back at Issac and smile, watching him jam to the music. "Look at that, Brandon, an alien who loves music..."

"I love music," Brandon says with a smile toward Christian, "Oh, yeah. You do. Hey Issac you know the words?"

Issac shakes his head, yes, gives a peace sign as Christian turns down the music. "I was there, at Woodstock. Joplin ad Hendrix were the best. You know Joe and the Country Fish? They were out of this world... close friends," Issac responds with a wider smile.

"We're heading for a war, little brother. Let's get ready," Christian says, staring, envisioning ahead... Issac begins singing, "Well common all of you big strong men uncle sam needs your help again, he got himself in a terrible jam, way down yonder in Vietnam, put down your books and pick up a gun we're gunna have a whole lotta of fun... and"–Christian, Issac, and Brandon begin singing together, "its one, two, three what are we fightin for? Don't ask me I don't give a dam, the next stop is Vietnam, and its five, six, seven..."

Incoming text from Tommy–*everyone's starting to respond, athletes, performing arts, ninth, tenth, eleventh, twelfth grades, man, bro–the whole school!!! We're going to kick alien...*

"Brandi," Brandon says as they abruptly stop singing. "Brandi. We have to find her, bro.

Save her," Brandon says to Christian with an affirmative nod... "Do I have any powers, or anything?" Brandon asks.

"Yeah, right. You have trouble cleaning up your room," Christian sarcastically responds. "You have a power," Issac says, jumping in.

"He does? I just thought he was a weird little brother," Christian says with a chuckle. "He has power," Issac says again. "But, he has to find it for himself. He was designed for… power… But not the kind you think…"

"How do you know so much about this topic, Issac? Something you learned at Woodstock?" Christian asks, becoming suspicious.

"You could say that. You know at Woodstock the whole theme about that festival was Peace…" Issac says, adding, "You have that power, Brandon, peace and love…"

"So, Brandon has the power of peace and love. Really? So, we're going to fight Reptilians and get Brandon's girl back with love?" Christian laughs.

"Exactly," Issac replies. "I can see it in his eyes, the power…"

"You know what, Issac? I don't even believe you were at Woodstock. You're probably just some average alien looking to get attention," Christian says, shaking his head in a dismissive manner.

"No, I'm not," Issac says, adding matter-of-factly, "I'm part Brandon's father…" Christian swerves the monster truck… Brandon turns back…

CHAPTER 15
Alien Woodstock–Ode to Brandi

In the attic, where time is crossing, Crystal and I find ourselves dancing, singing aloud to the beaming, vibrating music of the old CD player. I open my eyes, feeling as if I can change the world, I–*idealistic and innocent*, Maria Rivera… well, not innocent anymore. They, them took care of that. Yet, I dance in my attic as if I am dancing atop of the world with Crystal dancing in her alien costume, by my side, as she had all these years, through time… She had never left the side of that window, staring upward, with her heart, her dream she stayed connected to me as I vanished upward… into that tunnel.

I glance at myself in a dusty, cobwebbed aligned antique full-length mirror in the corner of the attic, with the single light bulb with a dangling chain, swinging, swaying back and forth. Gazing at the path I chose, my sexy cheerleader outfit, accepting to take on a journey to another distant universe of who I am, I began to understand, this moment in time was the destination of my choice, my path in which I gained two beautiful sons… and found myself, my real self, not perfect, not distant, yet aligned like the cobwebs of time–with the universe, in synchronization with the movement of space, time… *Einstein was right… Time is an illusion…* Abhijit Naskar the author of Love, God, & Neurons said, "he found himself by getting lost." Maybe, just maybe, I got lost, too, in a world of passion, love, hopes, and dreams of another universe.

"People like us who believe in physics know that the distinction between past, present, and future is only a stubbornly persistent illusion…" Albert Einstein. He believed that both the future and the past are unchangeable and connect exactly the way they were meant to be…

Hence, I am dancing in a skimpy cheerleader outfit, having taken a walk on the wild side, years ago, to yet, once again, strut against community self-constraints, to be, well, me... that part of time that was meant to be... I dance... with Crystal mirroring my movements in the mirror of that antique universe–in the corner of the attic.

We fall down, dancing, laughing. I help her up. "You're so stoned," I say to her. "So are you!" She cries back. I notice something else in the bin, another memory. I go over to the bin, reach in, and take the memory out–RED ROSARY BEADS. I stare at them, hold them to my chest as a cast filled trance flows from my eyes. Crystal goes over and looks back into the bin, too. She laughs, reaches in, and takes out the blue metallic sunglasses. She puts them on - *2001. The West Side of Manhattan, in the bind, according to Einstein*–Crystal is wearing the blue metallic sunglasses. I am dancing, wearing my pink thong and my straw cowboy hat... Smoke permeates our West Side Manhattan Apartment, looking through the sunglasses, Crystal sees Grey Aliens appear around us. "Maria!" She cries out as their long grey fingers, their hands wrap around me and pull me toward the open window... the Green Haired Zombie Soccer Player appears within the smoke. She takes hold of me, pulls me away from the aliens, who disappear out the window...

Crystal sees the Zombie guide me over to my bed, place me seductively down upon it, beginning to caress me, getting on top of me as I gaze upward seeing people, aliens watching us–I wrap my legs around her, on top of me, as she kisses the side of my neck, my head arches back, my toes curl... my body shakes in a sensual, tingling explosive exhilaration...

The tall man in the grey suit, the one with captivating grey-yellow eyes, emerges from the smoke, slowly manifesting behind Crystal as I turn and glance over toward them. He begins to ShapeShift to a REPTILIAN ALIEN.

The UFO operating room, aboard the ship. Crystal and I are upon metallic tables, encircled by aliens, Grey's and Reptilians. Our wrists and legs are spread out, on our backs, bound by blue metallic straps along with our foreheads, unable to turn our heads, our eyes wide open with large needles poised over us. Dr. Dragon and Issac stand by us; needles in hand as the tall Reptilian Alien gets off of me... "Man, that pot is strong," I hear Crystal echo out, tied to the table near me... "It's not the pot, Crystal... It's real," I cry back through a haze...

In another dimension, Julius, cautiously, walks toward our apartment, on the *West Side,* down the hallway, approaching our apartment door. The Green Haired Zombie is dead out in the hallway. He notices her head, twisted around her body. He nonchalantly steps over her and goes up to the door. He reaches into his pocket and unlocks the door with the key he found at the bus stop. Opens it - Julius walks in. He sees me partially awake in my bed, clasping upon my RED ROSARY BEADS and Crystal, lying partially unconscious leaning up against the wall by the open window. He moves toward her, turns, picks up the straw cowboy hat up off the floor, puts it on, and clasps upon the telescope pointed out the open window. Gazing through it, he sees in the night's sky a UFO, hovering above the Hudson, crossing my sight of this image in the new morning's sun…

He smiles. "I'm a good tracker," he says to himself, focusing in on the object. As the sun rises, he fades with colors of the dawn into another dimension with Crystal awakening… seeing me in my bed, clothing upon the red Rosary beads, my eyes opening in fear… The sound of a truck's horn echoing, propelling us back through time to the present, with the grandfather clock moving forward again, ticking…

I lift myself up off the floor of the attic alongside Crystal, taking off the blue metallic sunglasses. We gaze at each other. We found the answers, or so we thought, looking at each other without a word, knowing, not wondering. I had *my own version* of what Crystal saw, although we traveled through time together, me, in my cheerleader outfit, and Crystal, in her alien one.

Clasping upon my rosary beads, I say to her, "There were two kinds of aliens that took me, that night, Grey's and Reptilians. They didn't seem to like each other… You were there, too, and another woman on the other side of us. She was strapped down on another table. Her mount was gagged with some kind of instrument as she struggled to break free, looking over to me for help…

"What did they do to her?" Crystal replies, remaining on the floor, stunned, looking up.

"You were there, don't you remember?" I add.

"No. I'm confused. I didn't even realize I was there with you…"

"They used an instrument to cut open the young woman's skull. I could see them, the Reptilians, lift out her brain, Crystal…"

"What did they do with it?"

"They cut it up and gave it to each Reptilian standing behind us. They ate each piece. Then they came toward me. A Reptilian got on top of me and… Another one came toward me with a long needle. He inserted it in me. It was Dr. Drago. Someone else we know was there."

"Who?" Crystal asks.

I clasp tighter upon my rosary beads. "Crystal, there was a Reptilian alien on top of you, too? Don't you remember? You were screaming. I tried to break free and help you but then, then there was this bright Flash of Light. I found myself floating upward through some kind of… tunnel. The it all happened, the needle, the pain. It's all coming back to me…"

"Are you sure it wasn't just the pot?" Crystal says, shaking her head.

"No. It was real," I reply, adding to myself, "DeJa vu…" The grandfather clock strikes a long, strange, loud, resonating, eery reverberating tone.

"How long do you think we've been up here?" Crystal asks.

"Long enough. We better go," I reply, taking hold of Crystal's metallic sunglasses. "Go where?" Crystal asks, finally rising, yet, appearing more confused.

I go over and carefully placing the Rosary beads and the sunglasses back into the bin. Closing the bin, I respond, "To the future," "We have to get to the West Ridge. Everything is converging up there."

"How do you know?" Crystal asks.

"I just do…" I turn, noticing my white boots by the antique full length mirror. Grabbing hold of them, I put them on, push them in place, turn, and gaze at myself in the mirror wearing my sexy cheerleader outfit, my sheer, white, *booty shorts.*

"Well, that ought to do it," I say to Crystal.

"Do what?" Crystal responds, adding, "Attract whatever it is you're looking for?"

I smile. The house begins to shake from a force above us—ONCOMING UFO'S flying overhead. "Let's go…" "I have to change," Crystal says. "No time," I reply as the house shakes with more force and the horses whinny out in the corral… I pull on the chain—turn off the light.

"Christian! Brandon!" I cry out, running down the hall, looking into their rooms—empty. "Maybe they left," Crystal says.

We run down the stairs. The house is empty. I fling open the front door and walk out onto the front porch with Crystal closely following. I notice my truck is gone.

"I can't believe they took my truck. They're in so much trouble," I say, moving toward the corral. "With the aliens?" Crystal asks, looking up, seeing more fly overhead.

"No. With me," I say, angrily, adding, "No one touches my truck." I fling open the gate to the corral. Crystal immediately notices.

"Oh, no. I'm not riding any horse, again," She pauses, back up.

"It's the only way to get there, Crystal. Come one, get on," I say, throwing saddles on two of the horses, first, Silver, my horse, and second, Blaze, Crystal's destiny…

"There is no way I am getting on that horse," Crystal barks again. "His name is, Blaze."

"I don't care what his name is…" A low flying UFO startles Crystal, flying over her and swerving upward. "Okay, I'll get on…" Crystal attempts to mount Blaze with me holding onto the reigns. "Hold him still," Crystal says, struggling to get on."

"I am," I reply, adding, "He's just jumpy. He never had an alien ride him before." "Very funny," Crystal replies in her alien costume. Finally upon him, I jump on top of Silver in my cheerleader outfit and we take off, galloping out of the corral of the past and onward toward our future of our destinies across the ranch and into the desert toward the West Ridge…

"I can't believe we're doing this!" Crystal cries out, adding, "Don't you dare post pics…"

Brandon has his phone pointed toward the West Ridge as they race through desert with his brother driving and one of his fathers in the back seat. He sits in silence, not knowing what to believe as he clicks and captures pictures of the mountain range, wondering, just wondering.

Who is he? What is he? And, most importantly, out of all the unanswered questions, "What is Brandi's answer? Will she go to the prom with him?" He wonders, lowering his phone.

"You still with us, bro?" Christian asks. "You're not shaken up by what Issac said, are you?" Issac turns away, gazes out the window.

"No. It's not his fault. I'm just more concerned about Brandi, right now…" Brandon replies, glancing down at his phone. Text from Tommy–"We're almost there… Where r u?"

Brandon–"Coming… Will b there…" Christian turns off the music. A bright light of a UFO approaches. Christian notices.

"So, Brandon, your girl, the one they abducted, did you notice anything unusual about her?" Christian asks, gazing at the oncoming UFO.

Brandon, turns, envisions Brandi climbing up behind the waterfall– her Tiger Stripes. "Why?" Brandon answers.

"They're trying to connect their lost souls with God, through the use of the energy of Dark Matter," Christian says, adding, "Your girl might be one of… them."

"Brandi is not an alien. She's just a girl from school," Brandon responds upset.

"Not just a girl, Bro. She's the love of your life, right?" Christian returns with a smile. "Ah, the love of your life," Issac responds, awakening from the back.

"Do you have a love of your life, Issac? Or are test tubes your thing," Christian jabs. "What does the connection with souls have to do with Brandi," Brandon's asks. "How close did you get to your girl?" Christian says, sympathetically, "Did you…"

Brandon remained silent. "That close," Christian says, looking at the UFO hovering before them. "Brandon, don't you see? They took her because of you. She must be some kind of key, a piece of their Dark Matter equation… They're using her as bait, to lure you in. Remember? Remember when we used to go fishing? We always used that special kind of bait? Well, they don't know who they're messing with…" Christian swerves–pulls the truck over in a cloud of dust. "I'll show those…"

"What are you doing?" Brandon asks with Issac appearing concerned in the back as Christian jumps out of the truck, grabs the duffle bag out of the back bed, tosses it over his shoulder and begins angrily walking toward the hovering UFO with the alien gazing through the window, from above the Baltic Sea, staring at Christian through an oval window.

"You're time to fly, little brother!" Christian, staring defiantly at the alien, cries back. "What's he doing?" Brandon asks Issac.

"I think he's going to confront them, they…" Issac responds with Christian standing unrelenting beneath the hovering UFO. He pauses, still glancing up at the UFO as a beam shines down upon him, the same beam that shined down upon Brandi. He smiles, unzips the duffle bag.

"Let's Rock "N" Roll…" He says, clasping upon a weapon from the bag. Music comes on from inside the truck–*Woodstock. Raising his fist, Christian is pulled up into the BEAM OF LIGHT as Brandon gets out of the truck and watches… "Christian!"*

Issac climbs up into the passenger side of the truck. "Come on, Brandon. We have to get to the West Side," Issac says to him, standing, looking up to an empty, dark, star-filled sky.

Brandon, slowly, turns toward him. "It will be alright. Your brother can take care of himself. Trust me. Trust God, Brandon…" Brandon hesitates, but nods. He goes around and gets into the driver's side with the music from Woodstock still playing. He climbs in, clasps upon the wheel. "Your time to drive, little brother," Issac says with a smile, echoing Christian, adding, "He believes in you… And so do I…" Issac says, giving an affirmative nod while gesturing to the wheel. Brandon orientates himself to the control panel of the truck, envisioning the control panel of the DOME… He firmly places his hand upon the stick shift. Issac nods again and says, "Let's Rock "N" Roll…" Brandon shifts, presses on the accelerator, and takes off… speeding away.

"Are you really my father?" Brandon asks with a determined look to rescue Brandi. "In a Biological sense, yes…" Issac says, gazing ahead.

"So, that's why you came to our Ranch? To see me?" Brandon affirms. "I came to watch after you and…" Issac attempts to explain.

"And who?"

"Your mother… Do you know anything about your grandfather?" Issac says, adding, "Never mind… Let's go get your girl." Issac turns back on the music.

"Let's do it," Brandon says with a responsive affirmative nod, going even faster.

Music Blasting–*"Well it's one, two, three, what are we fight'n for, don't ask me I don't give a damn, next stop is Vietnam…"*

Maria and Crystal riding horses. "I can't believe you talked me into this…" Crystal struggles to control Blaze, galloping alongside Maria and Silver across the desert.

"Well, this wasn't something I envisioned doing today… You and your pot," Maria says, gently kicking Silver to gallop faster with Blaze keeping up, following.

"There is something I have to tell you," Maria calls out, clasping upon the reigns of their destiny. "I've been

"What? That you're an alien?" Crystal jests, barely holding on. "Yes," Maria says.

Crystal pulls back on the reigns, forcibly bringing Blaze to a. Full stop. "What the…"

Maria pulls back gently on Silver's reigns, turns, faces Crystal upon her horse, upon the desert, their moment in time where everything past, present, and future crosses.

"I've been meaning to tell you for years. But, I had to figure everything out… what happened that night, what I am, what I will become…" Maria says, gazing upward at the stars and UFO's, bright oval lights, passing overhead. "My mother told me as a child, but only once. As I grew up, I slowly forgotten what she said. My father was focused on some kind of mission. He included me on every trip, every quest he ever took. He tried to open my eyes to the universe and the secrets of Matter and Dark Matter, and fill those *Black Hole*s of the wondering part of my mind. Yet, everything in my life got sucked in, no light, no answers, no hope, until now."

"I'm not sure, I know what you're talking about…"

Brandon, as a child, climbs down into the tunnel upon the metal ladder. He approaches his grandfather at the center–illuminated shells of lights upon the walls, wearing a white coat and old-style googles. He turns toward Brandon and smiles–A BLUE AURA.

"Brandon isn't the only one, who is a hybrid. My father… my father was a Nordic." "What's a Nordic?" Crystal asks, adding, "From Sweden?"

"If you count Sweden from another galaxy, yes. They're a type of higher-level alien…" "Come on, Maria. Really? You're telling me this, now…" UFO's in a collage of light pass low overhead. Crystal looks up. "…with some kind of clashing alien type of armageddon about to begin?"

"Just thought you should know, before we get further into this," Maria says, turning Silver around, back toward the West Ridge, galloping off with Blaze trotting by their side and Crystal more firmly gripping her reigns.

"Is there anything else, you'd like to tell me before we face an army of aliens?" Crystal asks, sarcastically.

"Well, there is… you know that guy, the one you really liked at the Lobster Trap from the Jersey Shore?"

"Yeah, what about him?" Crystal ask, kicking Blaze into a gallop, a little farther ahead of Maria and Silver to face her. "What happened?"

"He and I…" Maria says with a slight smile in the wind and twirling dust. "Oh come on, Maria! You slept with the him! I was in love with him!" Maria kicks Silver into a fast paced run… Disappearing into a haze of dust.

"Oh, no…" Crystal shouts out, controlling Blaze and kicking him into a faster pace to catch up. "No you didn't, girl…"

Near the West Ridge, seeing a haze of various colored lights hovering above it, Brandon brings to the truck to a cautious slow speed, turning off the headlights.

"Why is all this happening, Issac?"

"There's a theory, just a theory, because of your genetic DNA and your connection to Dark Matter, with a key… your girl, Brandi, they can unlock the key to the universe and thus connect with the Higher Entity. There, you know, now," Issac says as Brandon stops the truck.

"Brandi is a key? She's just a cheerleader," Brandon says with a concerned look. "She's more than that, Brandon. She's also a daughter to a special kind of Reptilian, a

kind that can manage an adapt to live on earth. Everything around us, around you, is like a puzzle. Remember what we talked about when we watched, Ancient Aliens?"

"Which episode?" Brandon pauses, beginning to open the truck's door.

"The one that investigated the cross-over link between DNA… and matter throughout the universe in relation to Dark Matter and its force–Dark Energy, the one that's forcibly expanding the universe," Issac says, adding, "You seem calm for someone who just found out his love of his life is an alien Reptilian."

"I'm made up of three kinds of different alien species DNA, my girlfriend is a feared Reptilian alien…" "Half Reptilian…"

"Half Reptilian… my brother's an alien warrior and you, you Issac are a Grey alien, a part of my DNA mixture that was apparently injected into my mother after she was abducted a couple of decades ago. And you know what the most amazing and hard to believe part of all of this?" Brandon asks, turning toward Issac.

"What?" Issac asks, shaken, fearing Brandon, partially *shifts* into a Grey… "You were at Woodstock… How cool is that?" Brandon opens the door all the way and gets out. He looks up. Sees UFO's beginning to align above the canyon… He nods toward them. "Let's Rock "N"

Roll…" Issac gets out, goes and stands by his side. They gaze into the dark canyon below.

"Your grandfather, Brandon was a wise and kind man. I knew him. I met him. They, them, knew him. That's why they tracked your mother in college. Because his genes are a part of her… He created a lab and experimented with Dark Energy, a bridge between humans, aliens, and the Higher Entity. He hoped to create peace between all the species, a collaboration to discover far off parts to he universe…" Issac echoes, gazing up… "The universe, Brandon. It doesn't matter if you're rich or poor—you can always look up…"

Brandon gazes upward, toward the lights hovering above the canyon and the vast amount of bright stars beyond them. "Why do you think the universe is so big?"

"Don't know. We just know it all began as something as small as an acorn. Then, then it grew, amazingly large and powerful…" Issac looks down as Brandon follows. Issac looks into his eyes and says, "It's inside you, Brandon. You just need to grow, too, like that acorn."

"What's inside me?" Brandon asks, shaking his head, glancing around and above him. "What everyone is searching for, even us aliens…" Brandon says, slowly ShapeShifting

into a Grey. "What?" Brandon asks, again looking at him in his eyes.

"God, Brandon. God…" Issac says, fully shifted to a Grey. "We're all searching for Him, even those who don't know Who they are searching for… It's like an anomaly in physics. It doesn't make any sense and, yet, it is true. Jesus is true. He is Truth… and you have a mission, and it all began because your mother made a choice; her right choice, her chosen choice—a long, long time ago…

"I can't believe you talked me into this!" Crystal cries out, clinging to the reigns of Blaze, trying to hand on, appearing disheveled in her alien costume. "You had to be a cheerleader!"

"A sexy cheerleader!" I affirm back, gently kicking Silver to run faster, the wind blowing back my long hair, the short shorts riding up my bottom—appearing like a thong. "It was meant to be… taking a walk down that path of the wild side and you, stepping into the persona of a…

"Aliens," Brandon says looking up at the hovering lights. Issac turns toward the Blue Dome's Light—Brandon turns, sees the bright blue light, and nods to Issac…

Tommy, in the middle of the desert, sits atop a minibike with seven-hundred students alongside of him on various vehicles, minibikes, motorcycles, dune buggies, jeeps. Tommy looks up at the passing UFO's overhead.

"It's happening," Tommy says to the students alongside of him. "The West Ridge… We're going in… He raises his fist, signaling to the students to follow him. The students rev up their vehicles in unison–DUST–They take off across the desert toward the West Ridge… Brandon smiles, gazing up at the UFO's as they walk toward the Dome…

"You know what, Issac?" Brandon says, not wavering from his glance. "What's that, Brandon?" Issac asks.

"I feel like time is crossing and… Woodstock is about to begin…" *Music from Woodstock… Images of the students racing across the desert… The UFO's hovering…*

The UFO, that abducted Christian, lands in the middle of the desert–by the carcasses of cattle. A DOOR OPENS–Christian exits with his duffle bag, dragging dead aliens by a rope.

"I'm coming for you, little brother," Christian says, adding, "Payback is a… Here comes my calvary." Air force jeeps approach Christian. He gets into one of them, letting go of the rope. Soldiers place the bodies of the aliens into a large truck–HAZARDOUS WASTE with an image of an Alien with a Red X detailed on the side. One soldier in the truck turns toward Christian.

"Where to, Captain?"

"The West Ridge. Every breed of alien is heading there…" Christian says, reloading one his large guns. "Time to Rock "N" Roll…" The soldier nods, gets on the radio, and transmits–"We're heading to coordinates, Bravo one, zero, two eighteen. ETA–Fifteen minutes."

"Roger that…" A voice transmits back.

"We're going in," Christian adds to himself, "To get Brandon's girl…" The soldiers and Christian drive off–toward the West Ridge– *Yasgur's Farm of the Present.*

Brandon and Issac stand before the door of the Blue Dome. Brandon hesitates to open it. "What's the matter?" Issac asks, reaching out for the handle.

"Issac, were you the only alien at Woodstock?" Issac just smiles. "That's what I thought," Brandon says, glancing up at the varying UFO's, pushing the door open…

BRIGHT LIGHT... HUMMING SOUND. Brandon and Issac enter the Dome. The lights on the control panel are lit, flickering brightly in different coded shades of colors as if messages are being transmitted in a secretive dark web code, yet, not of this planet... No sign of Dr. Drago.

Issac stares at the control panel, approaches it. "It's some kind of messaging... Oh, my.

They're all coming..."

"Who?" Brandon asks as they move in synchrony toward the lit reflective exploding of multi-ray of unusual flickering coded colors as if in songs... dancing upon their brows.

"Everyone. Every type of alien from this galaxy and others... A Mega-Woodstock." Issac turns toward Brandon. "All the top.... Singers."

"Just like Woodstock. They didn't know everyone was going to converge like that," Brandon says moving closer to the panel, adding, "Can we stop it?"

"You can't stop your destiny, Brandon," Dr. Drago says, in a powerful resonating tone, emerging from the shadows. "I knew you'd come back. It's time for your final exam."

"Stay away from him, Drago. He knows what you are, now," Issac says, getting between them. "He's always known who I am," Drago replies, moving forward, lifting his Reptilian Hand toward the panel, orchestration the rhythm as a conductor of an unseen, quasi multidimensional orchestra of quantum vibrating particles, streaming through the universe converging upon earth.

"It's time, Brandon," Dr. Drago says, moving closer to Issac, facing him.

"You want a showdown, right here, right now?" Issac says in his alien form as Dr. Drago ShapeShifts to a large Reptilian. "Do what's right, Brandon. Draw upon what's in you. Don't fear. Don't blink. Be powerful..." Issac says, not yielding, nor swaying from the towering Drago over him. "Be brave, Brandon. Your grandfather was brave..."

"Yes. He was, until... I interceded. But, now is your time, Brandon. The inferior Grey is right. You need to draw from that energy Source, Dark Matter beating within Dark Energy and transfer this quantum realm to trigger the electromagnetic fields around earth. Everyone is in position, getting ready for the transfer of power... a connection to the Higher Entity," Dr. Drago says, pushing Issac aside and standing before Brandon

"That's not the power within I am talking about," Issac says with a slight glance back from Dr. Drago as he gestures toward the copper hatch.

"The answer for all of us, Brandon, is contained with Dark Matter, down in the tunnel. Your grandfather knew. That's why he used this spaceship to spearhead the path to Dark Matter that makes up much of the universe. And yet, the only place on earth is coincidently underneath your grandfather's ranch, right down there, right within you reach. It is the key to controlling Dark Energy–the very force that is expanding the universe. Yet, what if the key can be controlled, contract the universe and turn back time itself? Shift what will be to that of what could be…" Dr. Drago says, placing his Reptilian hand upon Brandon's shoulder. "What could be, Brandon. Your star, Brandon. She can be… I agree. Be brave. Make the right choice…"

Brandon stares at Issac, slowly turns, and moves toward the copper hatch. "The answer to your 'what if' lies down in that tunnel, Brandon. Don't let you shooting star pass by. Now, is your time," Dr. Drago says with a powerful sense of encouragement. "You can do it…"

"Don't do it, Brandon. Don't let it control you," Issac says, transforming back to a rancher along with Dr. Drago ShapeShifting back to a teacher. "Look in the bag, Brandon. Look in the tunnel… The answer lies within," Dr. Drago says in a softer tone.

"The answer, Brandon, doesn't lie within that tunnel. It lies within you…" Issac says as Brandon clasps hold upon the handle of the copper tunnel, flinging it open, being engulfed in a blue beaming light. "Then I have nothing to fear," Brandon says, adding, "I'm going in…"

"Spoken like a true fighter pilot," Dr. Drago says with a mischievous smile.

"Brandon, No!" Issac cries out as Brandon turns, and steps down upon the metal ladder and into the tunnel… crossing dimensions of decades of time…

As a child, Brandon discovers the copper hatch in the Dome. Without hesitation, he opens it and climbs down, his using the metal ladder, deeper down into a cylindrical tunnel and into an open room with oval lights, aligning unusual blue metallic steel walls–the same as that of the researched blue piece of metal found in the jungles of Peru. His grandfather stands at the center, wearing a helmet, goggles, and a white researcher's coat. He holds a clip board, writing upon it. He pauses, turns, and smiles at Brandon. "It's almost time, Brandon. When that time comes, you need to discover what's throughout the universe," his grandfather says, walking over to him and placing down the clipboard. Stooping down, gazing into Brandon's eyes, his grandfather says, "What's within you…" The blue lights emanating around his grandfather fade as Brandon finds himself at the bottom of the metal runged ladder, staring into a grey darkness of a cold room, a faded moment in time.

Then… A flash of Light. A pulse. Brandon's eyes ShapeShift to that of a very bright blue. Light beams from him. He gazes toward yellow awakening oval lights illuminating the bunker of Dark Matter. He glances down at his arm, the tattoo of "Hybrid," begins to melt. Becoming fearful, he turns and climbs back up the ladder. THE COPPER HATCH SHUTS AND LOCKS.

Dr. Drago stands above the hatch, turns toward Issac by the control panel. "You didn't think it would be that easy, did you?"

"What are you doing?" Issac asks, moving toward him. "Unlock the hatch. Let him out," Issac calls out as Brandon calls out beneath it. "Let me out!"

Dr. Drago raises his Reptilian Hand, with an unseen force, pushes Issac across the room and into the chair by the control panel. Issac attempts to break free. "Everything had begun. Time is crossing. My kind, my dear Issac, will soon be in control of the most powerful force in the universe. They're here…"

"You're locking your own son in that tunnel with that amount of Dark Energy?" Issac says, still trying to break free from an invisible force holding him in the chair.

"Open the hatch! My arm is burning!" Brandon cries out, banging on it with is fist.

With his mind, Issac begins chasing the colors of lights on the control panel. Dr. Drago notices. "What are you doing?" Dr. Drago asks, concerned.

"I'm sending signals, too, to my kind…" Issac says controlling the control power. Dr. Drago raises his hand. "It's not working. How are you…"

Issac, bound by an invisible force to the chair, ShapeShifts to eyes of blue. "You seem surprised, Dr. Drago, that an inferior Grey has a gift within him. For a researcher, you're not that observant. We connected to

Dark Energy while we were serving your kind, playing a role, a part of building those pyramids in the Amazon, long ago…"

Dr. Drago cries out, "No!" Raising his hand becoming a bright glow of a purple light, sliding Issac across the room on the chair with roller wheels and into the wall.

"I am the one with power," Dr. Drago says, using a purple glow of an electromagnetic force upon Issac as Issac slowly gets up from the floor.

"Do you? You're searching for that connection with the ultimate power of the universe, and, yet, you have no soul…" Issac says, defiantly standing.

"Our son, Brandon, needs to grasp upon his destiny," Dr. Drago says with Brandon crying out in cries of pain–burning. "Open the hatch! I'm burning!"

"We're wrong. The genetics aren't working. He needs our help, Drago." Issac says attempting to move, yet, frozen with a haze of purple glow around him.

"And we need his," Dr. Drago replies, gazing down at the hatch.

"You live in darkness, to do this to your son," Issac says, finally breaking free.

"No turning back," Dr. Drago says, stooping down to the hatch. "Brandon, can you hear me?" "Let me out, it's burning!"

"Shooting stars pass by, quickly, Brandon. Don't miss your destiny, your Brandi. The connection with her is down there, in that tunnel. Stop running from who you are!"

Brandon looks down the metal rungs and descends back down into the tunnel, into a resonating pulsating fiery light. At the bottom of the metal rungs, he glides with an unknown force and stands at the center of the bunker as the aura of light around him burns brighter, like the sun, in an fusion of energy, a bright color blue… Brandon ShapeShifts to an alien of LIGHT. The oval lights upon the walls become brighter with a louder emanating humming sound. His skin illuminates quantum particulates of pulsating energy–A BLUE AURA–as the instruments on the control panel go dark and the Dome begins to shake.

Dr. Drago smiles and waves his hand toward Issac, releasing him from the invisible force. "Oh, thee of little faith," Dr. Drago says to him. "It worked?" Issac asks perplexed.

Dr. Drago nods as he hears more UFO's pass overhead. "They're here… I'm sure you can watch after Brandon, our son. I'm going to check on the other variable to our equation proposal. Dr. Drago vanishes. Issac, quickly, goes over and opens the hatch. "Brandon!"–BRIGHT BLUE EMANATING LIGHT. MUSIC FROM WOODSTOCK…

West Ridge–Night–Hundreds of UFO's fly overhead and hover above the canyon. The soldiers from the air force arrive with Christian, riding in the jeeps and air force vehicles with the HAZARDOUS WASTE images of an Alien with a Red X detailed on the sides. One emblem–*ALIEN HUNTERS*.

Maria and Crystal approach riding upon their horses, down into the valley below. "This is so crazy. It's too dark. I can't see anything," Crystal says.

The lights of the hovering UFO's above and around the canyon–LIGHT UP.

"Well, it's not dark, now," I say, looking up at my destiny, the future that I somehow sensed, years ago. "Let's keep going," I add.

"Where?" Crystal asks, gazing up at all the UFO's.

"Back to our apartment," I simply say, leading her into the canyon of our deepest dreams. "It's going to happen down there…"

"What?" Crystal asks, the horses in a walk, moving cautiously down a hill, a path toward what we reached out to in my attic–the future I reached out to within that bin of the past…

A BEAM OF LIGHT shines down upon Brandi tied upright to a post, anchored with metallic ropes by her wrists and arms outstretched, standing at the CENTER of the CANYON–where time is crossing, converging from a past to a future, dimensions of dreams, of thoughts, of laws of reality crashing upon unyielding jagged rocks of wishes spilled out upon the shores from the deepest part of our souls… wondering, just wondering…

"Brandi…" I shockingly whisper out. "Brandon's right. She's more than just a girl…" I say to Crystal as we make our way down into the canyon upon our horses, one measured and calculated, one abandoned from guilt and free… mirroring the balance of a universe.

Wearing Rocco's Football Jersey–#77, Brandi gazes up into the blinding light pulsating down upon her with the UFO's moving to a lower, closer altitude–hovering, as my thoughts and fears for two decades. I found myself not wanting to run, anymore. I wanted to fight back to that night they took me, they, them…

Getting off Silver, I run up to Brandi in my cheerleader outfit a chose, years ago, with Crystal, dressed as an alien, closely following by my side. Standing next to her, sensing her own fear, I cast out all the darkness within me and gaze up into the bright light beaming down upon Brandi, raise my arms, my fists, and shout, "Take me! I am the one you want! Take me!" The light dims as the UFO's rise to a slight higher altitude. Brandi turns to me and says, "What's going on? One minute I'm at practice and the next... I'm here. Why am I tied up like this?" Brandi attempts to break free as I stare up into the UFO's moving into a calculated formation.

"I think they're getting ready for something..." I say, attempting to undo her bonds, and yet, in a strange way, as dimensions of time crossing; my own, as I grip upon my pen within the journal of my mind. "They're too tight," I say out loud. I can't undo them," I add, frustrated with the inner transcriptions of my thoughts, wrapped around darkness, as other lights of UFO's begin one by one to beam in different colors of lights down upon her... echoing varying versions of my self. "Who are you?" Brandi asks me, still struggling with her bonds. "Don't worry. I won't let them take you..." I respond, thinking, Who am I? A question I've been asking myself for two decades. "I'm Brandon's mother," I finally reply out, attempting to calm her.

"Why are you dressed like that?" She asks... another question asked, during that period of time I wanted to explore the universe. "This is what I was wearing when I got abducted by... them... I'm trying to figure things out. Long story..." I say to her.

"So, you know how to get me out of this. You got out, right?" she says. "It's going to be alright, Brandi. I won't leave you. Yes. I'll get you out..." I look up. Dr. Drago is approaching. "Drago," I say to myself, turning toward him. "I told you not to trust him," Crystal adds.

A bright light from one of the UFO's suddenly brightly shines down, targeting me, as students begin to arrive, encircling the ridge. Tommy sitting upon his minibike–notices me in my cheerleader outfit. "Wow. Brandon's mom is really hot..." A few students take my picture with their phones. "I wouldn't check instagram for a while, "Crystal sarcastically says, noticing Dr. Drago moving closer–*the darkness within me.*

"I'm finally starting to put everything together," I say to Crystal while watching him. "I'm beginning to remember..."

"Good. Because I'm beginning to feel a little strange being dressed as an alien in front of other…" Crystal says as Dr. Drago stands, now, directly before me.

"Allow me," Dr. Drago says with a simple wave of *his Reptilian Hand,* releasing Brandi from her bonds with *a wave* of all the repressed memories within me–symbolically *held within a shallow gasp of a terrified silence…*

Crystal moves closer to Brandi, looks into her eyes. "It's you…" she says, beginning to tear as Brandi connects with a genetic, yet, spiritual form toward her… mother. "Mom?" She replies back as Dr. Drago orchestrates with a wide smile and me, well, with another gasp of shock. "It's true?" I echo out as they hug within the forefront of Brandon appearing–coming toward us…

Seeing the UFO's align more in a definitive formation, appearing to make their move toward Brandi with lights flickering, as with the keyboard, upon her and Brandon's excitement upon seeing her reflecting amidst the bright lights, I turn toward Dr. Drago. "Why don't you just take me. You did it once before…" I finally utter out the truth trapped within me, spilling out like the other emotions from my East Side… "Take me," I pleaded to him, adding, "Leave Brandi and my son alone… please," knowing, somehow, Dr. Drago is the Mastermind Maestro of all the hovering lights of the UFO's in the sky.

"The girl is a Nexus between your son and the flow of Dark Matter cascading upward–toward the ships," Dr. Drago says, glancing toward Brandi and briefly upward. "Your purpose has already risen. Now, it's time for their's…" Dr. Drago turns as Brandi turns toward Brandon, releasing from the hug of Crystal, and focuses in on him moving toward her.

"What kind of Nexus? What are you talking about?" I ask him.

He gestures toward the sky, toward the ships, and says, "They've come from millions of light years away for… the powerful unique energy that is within you son…"

Brandon smiles at Brandi, locked in a stare, being beamed in… I was– upward–into the tunnel of the ship that night…

"And that girl, that girl, is the key to unlocking what's within him as a vortex centered Black Hole, connecting the energy source with the stations of the ships, positioned, right now, toward both of them. All that is missing is…"

"Is what?" I ask with a deeper gasp, looking up, remembering…

"For Brandon to realize who he is…" Dr. Drago says with a wider smile, yet, sterner look down toward Brandon, adding, "He's the only one who can make it all begin…"

As Brandon gets closer to Brandi, and I gaze toward my son, wondering, just wondering, the answer of my search through the universe and the universe within myself lights up, an AURA OF AN UNUSUAL BRIGHT BLUE LIGHT SURROUNDS BRANDON, EMANATING FROM HIM. "I told you, you have God within you, my son," I whisper with a loud echo across the universe, shaking the ships to the very core above us.

"Ah, the Prodigal Son returns," Dr. Drago says, with an affirmative nod toward Brandon.

Issac, slowly, emerges from the light by Brandon's side, moving in a purposeful determined stride toward Dr. Drago.

"I was on that table next to you, Maria," Crystal says, adding, "I remember, too… All of this has been orchestrated by Drago…"

"I know, Crystal… I know…"

FLICKERING LIGHTS ABOVE THEM LIKE THE LAMPPOSTS ON CAMPUS YEARS AGO–THE ENTIRE CANYON LIGHTS UP BRIGHTLY.

Christian stands with the air force soldiers atop the ridge. He raises his hand toward Tommy and the students to, hold their positions, seeing even more UFO's arrive with the embedded strange symbols in the dirt beginning to light up and move in synchronization like a landing field, the same symbols around the entrance of the tunnel in the Peruvian Jungle.

Brandon stands before Brandi. The critical moment has just begun. He gazes into her eyes and says, "Well." "Well, what?" She asks with a slight gasp. "Well, will you go to the prom with me?" Brandon asks, reaching out his hand and touching her, leaning in with a kiss…

An enormous flood of energy shoots upward in bright beams of lights toward all the UFO's as the canyon shakes with a earthquake and sounds of thunder ring out in the distance.

Brandi wraps her arms around Brandon and kisses him back as a blinding light wraps around them within an energy field of Matter, Dark Matter, Energy, and Dark Energy ALL colliding at this critical moment…

Finally, breaking the release, the energy fields beginning to fade, Brandi, inches from Brandon's lips whispers, "Yes… I'll go to the prom with you."

Dr. Drago smiles and says, "Well done, Brandon. Well done. You finally captured your shooting star." Dr. Drago glances upward at all the ships as, one by one, they take off at high speeds into the universe, like shooting stars across the night. Issac appears next to Dr. Drago.

"So, did they get what they are searching for?" Issac says, looking up into the changing sky with the markings in the dirt beginning to fade with passing dust…

Dr. Drago watches the sky and replies, "Remember when we were at Woodstock, Issac? What was the message back then… You remember, don't you?" Issac looks back down, meeting Dr. Drago's powerful stare.

"Peace, love, and unity," Issac replies.

"Ah, peace and love… Blessed are the peacemakers, Issac, for they shall be called sons of God…" Dr. Drago says with a smile.

"Brandon gave them the connection with God? He gave them peace and love?" Issac says, stunned.

"There will be no more wars between us, Issac, any of our kind." Dr. Drago glances back up. "They know, now… Peace is the answer…" Dr. Drago looks back down at Issac, places his Reptilian Hand on his shoulder and says, "You're right. Jesus is the answer… The Truth."

Dr. Drago fades away with the partially visible markings in the dirt as if sand passing through the fingers of time…

As a stare out my bedroom window–toward those Grey lined mountains of our blessed spanning ranch… I put down my pen and close my journal. "I look at the title, Dimensions of Time." having crossed out the "u" in "Sun." My reflections through time have brought me to this critical moment… Brandon stands in the doorway with Christian by his side. I turn…

"Mom, how do I look?" Brandon asks in his BLUE tuxedo for the PROM.

I rise from my chair and go toward both my sons, my Nexus between the secrets far off in the universe and the ones within me. They are my answer to God's Call. Within Jesus, I found myself and it took an alien to teach me that. Strange how life is… And, Brandon got his answer.

"I got her these," Brandon says, lifting up a bouquet of flowers.

"I picked them out," Christian adds with a proud smile, adding, "It's time for you to fly, little brother. Let's go. I'll drive you there…"

"Did you rent a limousine?" I asks.

They both smile. "No. Something better…"

As I stand on the front porch with Silver and Blaze calmly back in the corral, Crystal walks out and stands by my side as I watch them get into my truck and drive off.

"Brandon looks so handsome… You loaned them your truck?" She asks.

"It's our truck," I respond, gazing Crystal into the eyes. "It's always been our venture, our search. Thanks for always being with me through all this time…"

Crystal smiles and hugs me. "Thank you, too, sista from another universe…"

A cloud of dust rises around the truck as they ride across the ranch in our monster truck with Christian driving. Brandon sits in his tuxedo, holding the bouquet of flowers, glancing out the truck window toward the Grey lined mountains…

Issac, suddenly, appears in the backseat, startling them. "What are you doing here?" Christian asks, slightly, turning.

"I'm accompanying you guys are our next mission. The last one was so much fun…" Issac replies, patting Brandon on the shoulder. "Now, be yourself, Brandon…"

A BRIGHT BLUE LIGHT EMANATES from a LARGE SPINNING BALL above the gym at the Senior-Junior Prom of Red Rock High School.

Tommy stands with a group of students by the side, watching a group of female students dance, including Brandi. He walks up to Brandon, holding a glass, seeing he is staring at Brandi.

"Why don't you just do it," Tommy says to him.

"I'm not sure," Brandon replies, adding, "I heard she has a boyfriend, some guy who can shoot off light…"

"So. It doesn't hurt to try, right? I mean, what can happened?" Tommy says with a smile. "You're right. I'm going in…" Brandon says, handing Tommy his glass.

"Spoken like a true fighter pilot…" Tommy replies with an affirmative nod.

Brandon cautiously walks up to Brandi dancing. She pauses, brushes back her hair, and turns… "Do you have something you want to ask me?" Brandi asks, placing her arms around him. "Yes… Do you want to dance with me?" Brandon responds as they begin to slow dance to a romantic song with cascading lights shining down above them at the center of the dance floor–FLICKERING.

A teacher approaches Mr. DeGenova, standing off by the side guarding the buffet and drinks from a fountain. They both glance over and watch Brandon and Brandi dancing beneath the lights in a passionate embrace.

"I never really understood why you would put our highest performing student on a long- term suspension," the teacher says to him.

"I had to," Mr. DeGenova replies.

"Policy?" The teacher asks.

"You could say that. You see the only way I could get Brandon to understand his… full potential and grow him emotionally, at the same time, was to shake things up a bit. So, I gave a friend of mine a call… He owed me one. In hindsight, I should have told my secretary, though."

"Brilliant. It looks like he's grown with his social skills. Good plan…" the teacher replies. "So, you're the one who orchestrated all of this," the teacher adds as Brandon and Brandi kiss amidst the mesmerizing, swirling lights of *THE DANCE WITHIN THE UNIVERSE.*

Mr. DeGenova smiles, turns away and says, "I'm just a high school assistant principal"–HIS EYES TURN TO AN INVERTED REPTILIAN YELLOW.

DIMENSIONS OF TIME-SYNOPSIS

On a dawn of a new day for New York and a young idealistic, astrophysicist NYU student, Maria Rivera, dimensions of time cross, opening up a quantum level journey that would unlock secrets of the universe in a quest to find a divine purpose embodied within the search for a Higher Entity for humans, alien-hybrids, and the Grey's, Nordics, and feared Reptilian aliens. With her close friend, Crystal, by her side through two decades of running from the alien abduction of *that night* by *they, them,* Maria gains courage to explore the universe held within the deepest parts of the passionate desires of her heart and ventures to discover her true calling through raising two sons, one; a fighter pilot on a mission, Christian, and the other; a brilliant high school student, Brandon, who is infatuated with a beautiful exotic young woman in his class. After being suspended for getting into a fight in attempt to take her to the prom, a strange, mysterious researcher from the jungles of the Amazon shows up at the family ranch in Arizona to tutor Brandon in which conflicts, subsequently, arise between two historically combative species of aliens, spanning centuries, whereby genetics weaved within Brandon's designed destiny, ultimately, come to fruition and collide during investigations into the existence of Dark Matter on earth that can create a possible bridge through a genesis-driven bond between Brandon and his infatuation in order to connect the *soulless* alien life forms with that Higher Entity - God - described in the Book of Enoch's citations of the Nephilim - *the Fallen Angels.*

www.ingramcontent.com/pod-product-compliance
Lightning Source LLC
Chambersburg PA
CBHW040826010826
48978CB00012BB/620